My
GOLD
·STORY BOOK·

TREASURE PRESS

First published in Great Britain in 1981 by The Hamlyn
Publishing Group Limited

This edition published in 1990 by
Treasure Press
Michelin House
81 Fulham Road
London SW3 6RB

ISBN 1 85051 407 0

The material in this book formerly appeared in
Giant All-Colour Storybook published by The
Hamlyn Publishing Group Limited.

Illustrations are by: Victor Ambrus Val Biro David Frankland
John Patience Peter Richardson John Speirs

50 749

Contents

The Enchanted Horse

I N the fair land of Persia, long, long ago, the first day of each year was kept as a time of great rejoicing, when people of all countries brought before the sultan any new or wonderful things they had. On one of these feast days a poor Indian came, and he claimed to have the most wonderful horse that had ever been made by man.

'I praise my horse,' said he, 'not for his looks, but for what he is able to do. He will carry me to any place I wish to visit, and if your majesty chooses, I will show you his power.'

'Go then,' replied the sultan, 'to yonder mountain and bring back to me a branch of the palm that grows at its foot.'

Mounting the horse, the Indian turned a peg in the creature's neck, and the next moment was carried into the air and out of sight. In less than a quarter of an hour he came back, bearing the palm branch in his hand.

Upon this, the sultan offered to buy the horse, but the Indian would not take money for it.

'I will take only your daughter in exchange for the horse,' he said, at which the officers standing round laughed aloud; but the prince, the son of the sultan, fearing his father might make the bargain, drew near and said, 'Sir, you surely will not insult the princess, my sister, by giving her in marriage to this vain fellow!'

'Son!' replied the sultan, 'it may be the man will take some other reward for the animal, which is so truly wonderful, that I do not wish any other prince to become the owner of it. But, before I bargain with him, I should like to see you try the animal.'

To this the Indian agreed, and the prince mounted; but, before the Indian had told him what to do, he turned the peg, and was carried high into the air.

'Sir,' cried the Indian, turning to the sultan in alarm, 'I pray you will not blame me should any harm come to the prince, your son. I would have told him all he should know of the working of the horse had he given me the chance. Unless he finds the second peg, he cannot return to the earth again.'

On hearing this, the sultan became greatly troubled, and the Indian, in order to calm him, continued, 'Have no fear, your majesty. The horse will carry him safely over sea and land, and should he fail to see the second peg, he has but to wish to be in a certain place, and the horse will even carry him there.'

'I hope that what you say is true,' the sultan answered, 'but, in case it is not, I shall keep you in prison until my son returns.'

Now, the prince, on finding the horse travel on and on, rising higher and higher all the time, tried his best to stop it. At last, after some searching, he found the second peg, which he turned. No sooner had he done this than the horse began to descend, and the prince at length found himself on the roof of a great palace. It was now quite dark, for the night had come, but after a time he found a small staircase, which led him to a small room, where lay several enormous servants fast asleep.

Passing these with great care, he entered another room, where, on a raised bed, lay a beautiful princess, and around her several women all sound asleep. Feeling that his only safety lay in begging the princess to protect him, he wakened her.

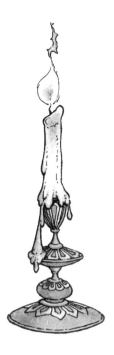

'Princess,' he said when her eyes were open, 'you see before you the son of the King of Persia, who finds himself in your palace, and at the mercy of your servants, unless you will have the goodness to help him.'

'Prince,' replied the lady, who was the daughter of the King of Bengal, 'have no fear. In this country you will find nothing but welcome. As you must be in need of food and rest, I will send some of my women to see to your comfort, and in the morning I will hear your strange story.'

Upon this the women led the prince to a large room filled with much beautiful furniture, and, while some got food for him, others made ready a bed, on which, after he had eaten, he lay down.

In the morning the princess dressed herself with more than usual care, for she already loved the handsome prince who had come to her in so strange a manner. As soon as she was ready, she said to a servant, 'go to the Prince of Persia, and ask if he is ready to receive a visit from me.' The prince, having heard the message, awaited her coming with great joy.

'Prince,' she said, as soon as the greetings were over, 'I came here because no one will come into this room. I pray you tell me to what I owe the pleasure of seeing you in my palace.'

The prince told her of the coming of the poor Indian to the feast of the New Year, of his wonderful horse, and of his wish to exchange it for the hand of the Princess of Persia. He told her, too, of his own fear lest his father should consent, and also of his rashness in leaving the ground without first having learned the working of the animal.

'At last,' he said, 'I found a second peg, and turning it, was soon brought down to the terrace on the roof of your palace. Creeping softly down the stairs and past your servants, I reached your room and wakened you. The rest of the story is known to you, and all that is now left for me to do is to thank you for your goodness, and to declare that you have already won my heart by your beauty and your kindness.'

On this, the princess, blushing with pleasure, answered, 'Prince, I have listened to your story with great interest, but I can hardly help shaking with fear when I think of your danger. It is well that the enchanted horse brought you to my palace. I do not, however, find myself able to believe that I have won your heart, for it is far more likely that you have given it to some fair lady of Persia.'

It was now time for dinner, and the princess, leading the way to a beautiful hall, sat down with the prince to a delicious meal.

'Prince,' said the princess, when dinner was over, 'you may now be thinking of returning to your own country; but you should not leave the kingdom of Bengal without first seeing the palace of the king my father.'

Now, though the Prince of Persia would gladly have done this, he felt he could not visit the father of the princess in the clothing he then wore. When he told the princess this, she replied that she would supply him with all he needed, feeling sure that if her father saw the Prince of Persia, he would allow her to marry him.

The prince, however, would not agree. 'If you will permit me,' he said, 'I will first return to Persia and let my father know of my safety; then I will come back, not as a stranger, but as a prince, and ask for your hand in marriage.'

Yet, as the princess seemed so little pleased to let him go, he stayed on and on until he had been two whole months in the kingdom of Bengal. Banquets and balls were given in his honour; but at last he resolved to set out for Persia and to take the princess with him.

Placing her on the enchanted horse, therefore, he mounted behind, turned the peg, and was quickly carried to the chief city of his father's kingdom. Here he left the princess in the care of the housekeeper, at one of his father's smaller residences on the outskirts of the town, and hurried off to the sultan, who had long thought him dead.

When the sultan had heard the prince's story, he ordered that all signs of mourning in the court should be put away, and declared that he would not only consent to the marriage, but that he would himself go and meet the princess whom his son so dearly loved.

Before setting out, however, he sent for the Indian, to whom he said, 'I kept you in prison in order to put you to death unless my

son returned in safety. I thank God he has so returned. Go, therefore, take your horse, and never enter my kingdom again.'

Now the Indian, having learned on his way from the prison about the princess whom the king's son had brought home, resolved, on leaving the palace, to carry her off. And this he did with little trouble, for the princess, thinking he had been sent to fetch her, mounted the horse with him, and was carried away over the heads of the sultan and the prince, who, though they saw her, could not help her.

The king returned in sorrow to the palace, but the prince, dressing himself as a priest, set out to find where she had been carried. and to save her from the wicked Indian, who meant to make her his wife.

But the princess, on learning what the Indian wished, would not listen to him; so he treated her with great violence, and one day, when he was more cruel than usual, she screamed so loudly that some horsemen passing by came to her aid.

One of these horsemen proved to be the Sultan of Cashmere, and he, hearing the princess's story, slew the Indian, and took her to his own palace, meaning to marry her himself, for he was much struck by her wonderful beauty.

Though he had not yet asked her consent, he ordered the rejoicings to begin at once; but the princess, having given her word to the Prince of Persia, would not marry the Sultan of Cashmere, and, in order to stop him from forcing her to do so, she pretended to go mad.

So wildly did she behave that the sultan sent for many doctors, none of whom, however, could cure her.

At last the sultan offered a reward to any doctor of any country who should restore the Princess of Bengal to health again.

Now it chanced that the Prince of Persia heard of this, and feeling sure the sick person must be his own lost princess, went to Cashmere. By the sultan's leave he entered the room in which she was sitting, and singing softly to herself of the prince to whom she had given her heart.

On seeing him she took him for another doctor, for his beard had grown very long, so she flew into a great rage. But the prince, speaking so that none but she could hear, told her who he was, and that he had come to save her. On this she grew quiet, and the prince, returning to the sultan, said he thought he could cure her if he were allowed to do it in his own way. 'But, sir,' he said,

'it would be of great help to me if I knew how the princess came to be in Cashmere, which is very far from her own country.'

To this the sultan replied that she had been carried there by an Indian on an enchanted horse, which he had put in his treasury because it was such a wonderful animal.

'That horse,' said the prince, 'is the cause of all the trouble. The princess has been enchanted by riding on it, and I am now sure I can cure her by the aid of the animal, if your majesty will order it to be brought out into the great square before the palace.'

The very next day the enchanted horse was placed in the square, and all the people and the nobles of the court stood around, to watch the new doctor cure the Princess of Bengal of her madness.

Dressed in rich garments, with jewels sparkling on her neck and wrists, the princess came from the castle, with a great many ladies, who helped her to mount the enchanted horse. In full view of the sultan and all his people she sat, while the pretended doctor walked three times round the horse, his hands crossed on his breast, and strange words coming from his lips.

Then, placing round the horse a great many vessels of fire he had ordered to be brought, he mounted behind the princess, who was quite hidden by the thick smoke, turned the peg, and, before any one knew what was happening, both of them were carried high into the air.

'Sultan of Cashmere,' cried the Prince of Persia, as they passed over his head, 'the next time you wish to marry a lady, you had better first ask her consent.'

The enchanted horse soon carried them back to Persia, where, as soon as possible, the prince and princess were married. The Sultan of Persia was quite willing, and the King of Bengal thought his daughter greatly honoured in being chosen by so brave a man as the prince had proved himself to be.

The Fox & the Rook

THE cawing of rooks filled the air as they swept across the pink sky in a black cloud towards their untidy homes in the treetops.

They were led by an old and greying bird whose word was law, and behind him came the older members of the family followed by the younger rooks who had been hatched in the spring. These were impatient young birds, proud of their strong young wings and throaty voices. Lagging far behind them was the most conceited young rook of all.

She had no need to hurry because she was confident that she could easily catch up whenever she wanted. As her wings flapped lazily her bright eyes spotted the open window of a house and she decided to investigate.

Swooping past the window she was delighted to see a table in the room beyond laden with delicious food. Turning awkwardly she looped backwards, flew through the open window and snatched up a large piece of beef. Her heart beating, with excitement she flew with her prize to a small clump of fir trees. The meat was heavy, and breathlessly she settled on a comfortable branch, her bright eyes sparkling with satisfaction and greed.

A dying sunbeam glanced through the branches and settled on something brown and furry among the pine needles and bracken at the foot of the tree. The brown patch moved silently forward and there, in the rose of the setting sun, was a fox.

It was rather early for him to be setting out for his night's hunting, but he was very hungry and when he looked up and saw the rook with the juicy piece of meat in her mouth his mouth watered with envy.

The rook glanced down at him with scorn. She thought the fox a rather common form of life. Why, he could not even fly!

DAVID FRANKLAND.

The fox concentrated his gaze upon the meat, his brain working quickly, his amber eyes alive and bright. At all costs, he decided, he must have the meat. His beautiful brush swayed gently and he licked his chops. Then he smiled up at the rook and said in a soft voice. 'What vision of beauty is this that I see?'

The rook cocked her head on one side and stared downwards, still holding the piece of meat firmly in her beak.

Then she heard the fox say, 'Surely, those beautiful wings must have come from a fairy nest! And those eyes, so soft and liquid to behold, so star-like and so gentle.'

The rook fidgeted a little and thought, 'Perhaps I was mistaken. The fox appears to be a most elegant and sensible fellow.'

The fox took a breath and went on, 'Never in all my travels have I seen such exquisite poise, such dignity. And her breast! surely the swans on the lake would be green with envy if they should see such soft and fairy-like lightness!'

The rook preened herself but still held tightly to her prize. She was longing to hear more and waited expectantly. The fox continued, 'That smooth beak, those dainty feet. This must be the wonderful rook that I have heard about.'

The rook took a step to right and left upon her perch but still held on to the meat. Then the fox muttered, 'Now, if only she could sing like the nightingales! But of course, with such outward beauty she probably cannot sing at all. What a pity! If only she could sing she would be the queen of them all.'

The conceited young rook could contain herself no longer. The fox, she decided, was a gentleman of taste and quality. She must show him that her voice was every bit as beautiful as her figure and colouring. She simply could not remain silent and she opened her beak as wide as possible. 'CAW! CAW! CAW!' she croaked, making the most ugly sound that ever was heard.

There was a sudden bark of excitement from the foot of the tree as the slice of juicy meat fell on to the ground. The fox pounced upon it instantly and gripped it between his strong jaws. As he ran off the rook screamed in fury, 'CAW! CAW! CAW! You wicked thief! Give me back my meat, CAW! CAW! You wicked thief!'

_____ *Men who flatter often have an ulterior motive.* _____

Rumpelstiltskin

I N a certain kingdom once lived a poor miller who had a very beautiful daughter. She was, moreover, exceedingly shrewd and clever, and the miller was so vain and proud of her that he one day told the king of the land that his daughter could spin gold out of straw. Now this king was very fond of money, and when he heard of the miller's boast his greed was excited and he ordered the girl to be brought before him. Then he led her to a chamber where there was a great quantity of straw, gave her a spinning-wheel and said, 'All this must be spun into gold before morning, if you value your life.'

She began to cry over her hard fate, when suddenly the door opened, and a funny-looking little man hobbled in and said, 'Good day to you my sweet lass, what are you weeping for?' 'Alas!' answered she, 'I must spin this straw into gold, and I don't know how.' 'What will you give me,' said the little man, 'to do it for you?' 'My necklace,' replied the maiden. He took her at her word and sat himself down to the wheel; round about it went merrily and, presently, the work was done and the gold spun.

When the king came and saw this he was greatly astonished and pleased, but his heart grew still more greedy and he shut up the poor miller's daughter again with a fresh task. Then she did not know what to do, and sat down once more to weep, but the little man presently opened the door and said, 'What will you give me to do your task?' 'The ring on my finger,' she replied. So her little friend took the ring and began to work at the wheel, till, by the morning, all was finished.

The king was again delighted to see all this glittering treasure, but still he was not satisfied and took the miller's daughter into a yet larger room, and said, 'All this must be spun tonight, and if you succeed, you shall be my queen.' As soon as she was alone the dwarf came in and said, 'What will you give me to spin gold for you this third time?' 'I have nothing left,' said she. 'Then promise me,' said the little man, 'your first little child when you are queen.' 'That may never be,' thought the miller's daughter, but as she knew no other way to get her task done she promised him what he asked, and he once more spun the whole heap of gold. The king came in the morning and, finding all he wanted, married her, and so the miller's daughter really became queen.

At the birth of her first little child the queen rejoiced very much and forgot the little man and her promise, but one day he came into her chamber and reminded her of it, and he said, 'I will give you three days' grace, and if, during that time, you tell me my name, you shall keep your child.'

Now the queen lay awake all night, thinking of all the odd names that she had ever heard, and dispatched messengers all over the land to inquire after new ones. The next day the little man came, and she began with Timothy, Benjamin, Jeremiah and all the names she could remember; but to all of them he said: 'That's not my name.'

The second day she began with all the comical names she could hear of, Bandy-legs, Hunch-back, Crookshanks and so on, but the little gentleman still said to every one of them, 'That's not my name.'

The third day one of the messengers came back and said, 'I can hear of no other name, but yesterday, as I was climbing a high hill among the trees of the forest where the fox and the hare bid each other good night, I saw a little hut, and before the hut burnt a fire, and round the fire danced a funny little man upon one leg and sang:

> 'Merrily the feast I'll make,
> Today I'll brew, tomorrow bake;
> Merrily I'll dance and sing,
> Rumpelstiltskin is my name!'
> My lady cannot play this game;
> For next day will a stranger bring.

When the queen heard this she jumped for joy, and as soon as her little visitor came and said, 'Now, lady, what is my name?'

'Is it John?' asked she.

'No!'

'Is it Tom?'

'No!'

'Can your name be Rumpelstiltskin?'

'Some witch told you that! Some witch told you that!' cried the little man, and in a rage dashed his right foot so deep into the floor that he was forced to lay hold of it with both hands to pull it out. Then he made off as fast as possible, while everybody laughed at him for having had all his trouble for nothing and for being called such a funny name.

The Kite, the Frog & the Mouse

T HERE was once much argument between a frog and a mouse as to which should be master of the fen, and many pitched battles resulted.

The crafty mouse, hiding under the grass, would make sudden attacks upon his enemy, often surprising him at a disadvantage.

The frog was stronger than his rival, however, and, hoping to end the dispute, challenged the mouse to single combat.

The mouse accepted the challenge, and on the appointed day the champions entered the field, each armed with the point of a bulrush, and both confident of success.

A kite chanced to be hovering overhead at the time, and seeing the silly creatures so intent upon their quarrel, she swooped suddenly down, seized them in her talons, and carried them off to her young.

DAVID
FRANKLAND.

United we stand divided we fall.

19

The Selfish Giant

EVERY afternoon, as they were coming from school, the children used to go and play in the giant's garden.

It was a large lovely garden, with soft green grass. Here and there over the grass stood beautiful flowers like stars, and there were twelve peach-trees that in the spring-time broke out into delicate blossoms of pink and pearl, and in the autumn bore rich fruit. The birds sat on the trees and sang so sweetly that the children used to stop their games in order to listen to them. 'How happy we are!' they cried to each other.

One day the giant came back. He had been to visit his friend the Cornish ogre, and had stayed with him for seven years. After the seven years were over he had said all that he had to say, for his conversation was limited, and he determined to return to his own castle. When he arrived he saw the children playing in the garden.

'What are you doing here?' he cried in a very gruff voice, and the children ran away.

'My own garden is my own garden,' said the giant; 'any one can understand that, and I will allow nobody to play in it but myself.' So he built a high wall all round it, and put up a notice-board

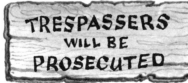

TRESPASSERS WILL BE PROSECUTED

He was a very selfish giant.

The poor children had now nowhere to play. They tried to play on the road, but the road was very dusty and full of hard stones, and they did not like it. They used to wander round the high walls when their lessons were over, and talk about the beautiful garden inside. 'How happy we were there!' they said to each other.

Then the spring came, and all over the country there were little blossoms and little birds. Only in the garden of the selfish giant it was still winter. The birds did not care to sing in it as there were no children, and the trees forgot to blossom. Once a beautiful flower put its head out from the grass, but when it saw the notice-board it was so sorry for the children that it slipped back into the ground again, and went off to sleep. The only people who were pleased were the snow and the frost. 'Spring has forgotten this garden,' they cried, 'so we will live here all the year round.' The snow covered up the grass with her great white cloak, and the frost painted all the trees silver. Then they invited the north wind

to stay with them, and he came. He was wrapped in furs, and he roared all day about the garden, and blew the chimney-pots down. 'This is a delightful spot,' he said, 'we must ask the hail to visit.' So the hail came. Every day for three hours he rattled on the roof of the castle till he broke most of the slates, and then he ran round and round the garden as fast as he could go. He was dressed in gray, and his breath was like ice.

'I cannot understand why the spring is so late in coming,' said the selfish giant, as he sat at the window and looked out at his cold, white garden; 'I hope there will be a change in the weather.'

But the spring never came, nor the summer. The autumn gave golden fruit to every garden, but to the giant's garden she gave none. 'He is too selfish,' she said. So it was always winter there, and the north wind and the hail and the frost and the snow danced about through the trees.

One morning the giant was lying awake in bed when he heard some lovely music. It sounded so sweet to his ears that he thought it must be the king's musicians passing by. It was really only a little linnet singing outside his window, but it was so long since he had heard a bird sing in his garden that it seemed to him to be the most beautiful music in the world. Then the hail stopped dancing over his head, and the north wind ceased roaring and a delicious perfume came to him through the open casement. 'I believe the spring has come at last,' said the giant; and he jumped out of bed and looked out.

What did he see?

He saw a most wonderful sight. Through a little hole in the wall the children had crept in, and they were sitting in the branches of the trees. In every tree that he could see there was a little child. And the trees were so glad to have the children back again that they had covered themselves with blossoms, and were waving their arms gently above the children's heads. The birds were flying about and twittering with delight, and the flowers were looking up through the green grass and laughing. It was a lovely scene, only in one corner it was still winter. It was the farthest corner of the garden, and in it was standing a little boy. He was so small that he could not reach up to the branches of the tree, and he was wandering all round it, crying bitterly. The poor tree was still covered with frost and snow, and the north wind was blowing and roaring above it. 'Climb up! little boy,' said the tree, and it bent its branches down as low as it could; but the boy was too tiny.

And the giant's heart melted as he looked out. 'How selfish I have been!' he said; 'now I know why the spring would not come here. I will put that poor little boy on the top of the tree, and then I will knock down the wall, and my garden shall be the children's playground for ever and ever.' He was really very sorry for what he had done.

So he crept downstairs and opened the front door quite softly, and went out into the garden. But when the children saw him they were so frightened that they all ran away, and the garden became winter again. Only the little boy did not run for his eyes were so full of tears that he did not see the giant coming. And the giant stole up behind him and took him gently in his hand, and put him up into the tree. And the tree broke at once into blossom,

and the birds came and sang on it, and the little boy stretched out his two arms and flung them round the giant's neck, and kissed him. And the other children, when they saw that the giant was not wicked any longer, came running back, and with them came the spring. 'It is your garden now, little children,' said the giant, and he took a great axe and knocked down the wall. And when the people were going to market at twelve o'clock they found the giant playing with the children in the most beautiful garden they had ever seen.

All day long they played, and in the evening they came to the giant to say good-bye.

'But where is your little companion?' he said: 'the boy I put into the tree.' The giant loved him the best because he had kissed him, and had not been afraid.

'We don't know,' answered the children; 'he has gone away.'

'You must tell him to be sure and come tomorrow,' said the giant. But the children said that they did not know where he lived, and had never seen him before; and the giant felt very sad.

Every afternoon, when school was over, the children came and played with the giant. But the little boy whom the giant loved was never seen again. The giant was very kind to all the children, yet he longed for his first little friend. 'How I would like to see him!' he used to say.

Years went by, and the giant grew very old and feeble. He could not play about any more, so he sat in a huge arm-chair, and watched the children at their games, and admired his garden. 'I have many beautiful flowers,' he said, 'but the children are the most beautiful flowers of all.'

One winter morning he looked out of his window as he was dressing. He did not hate the winter now, for he knew that it was merely the spring asleep, and that the flowers were resting.

Suddenly he rubbed his eyes in wonder and looked and looked. In the farthest corner of the garden was a tree quite covered with lovely white blossoms. Its branches were golden, and silver fruit hung down from them, and underneath it stood the little boy he had loved.

Downstairs ran the giant in great joy, and out into the garden. He hastened across the grass, and came near to the child. And when he came quite close his face grew red with anger, and he said, 'Who has dared to wound you?' For on the palms of the child's hands were the prints of two nails, and the prints of two nails were on the little feet.

'Who has dared to wound you?' cried the giant; 'tell me, that I may take my big sword and kill him.'

'No,' answered the child; 'for these are the wounds of love.'

'Who are you?' said the giant, and a strange awe fell on him, and he knelt before the little child.

And the child smiled on the giant, and said to him, 'You let me play once in your garden, today you shall come with me to my garden, which is paradise.'

And when the children ran in that afternoon, they found the giant lying dead under the tree, all covered with white blossoms.

The Wild Swans

FAR away, in a country where the swallows fly in our winter-time, there lived a king who had eleven sons, and one daughter, the beautiful Elise. The eleven brothers went to school with stars on their breasts, and swords by their sides; they wrote on golden pads with diamond pens, and could read either with a book, or without one; in fact, it was easy to see that they were princes. Their sister Elise used to sit upon a little glass stool, and had a picture-book which had cost half a kingdom. Oh, the children were so happy! But they were not to remain so for long.

Their father, the king, married a very wicked queen, who was not at all kind to the poor children. They found this out on the first day after the marriage, when there was a grand ball at the palace; for when the children played at receiving company, instead of giving them as many cakes and sweets as they liked, the queen gave them only some sand in a little dish.

The week after, she sent little Elise to be brought up by some peasants in the country, and it was not long before she told the king so many lies about the poor princes, that he would have nothing more to do with them.

'Away out into the world, and take care of yourselves,' said the wicked queen. 'Fly away in the form of great speechless birds.' But she could not make their transformation as disagreeable as she wished – the princes were changed into eleven white

swans. Sending forth a strange cry, they flew out of the palace windows, over the park and over the wood.

It was still early in the morning when they passed by the place where Elise lay sleeping in the peasant's cottage; they flew several times round the roof, stretched their long necks, and flapped their wings, but no one either heard or saw them; they were forced to fly away, up to the clouds, and into the wide world; so on they went to the forest, which extended as far as the seashore.

Poor little Elise stood in the peasant's cottage amusing herself with a green leaf, for she had no other plaything. She pricked a hole in the leaf and peeped through it at the sun, and then she fancied she saw her brothers' bright eyes, and whenever the warm sunbeams shone down upon her cheeks, she thought of her brothers' kisses.

One day passed exactly like another. When the wind blew through the thick hedge of rose-trees, in front of the house, she would whisper to the roses 'Who is more beautiful than you?' but the roses would shake their heads and say, 'Elise.' And when the peasant's wife sat on Sundays at the door of her cottage reading her hymn-book, the wind would rustle in the leaves and say to the book, 'Who is more pious than you?' 'Elise,' replied the hymn-book. And what the roses and the hymn-book said, was no more than the truth.

Elise, who was now fifteen years old, was sent for to return home; but when the queen saw how beautiful she was, she hated her even more, and would willingly have transformed her like her brothers into a wild swan, but she dared not do so, because the king wished to see his daughter.

So the next morning the queen went into a bath which was made of marble, and fitted up with soft pillows and the gayest carpets; she took three toads, kissed them, and said to one, 'settle yourself upon Elise's head, that she may become dull and sleepy like you.' 'Settle yourself upon her forehead,' said she to another, 'and let her become ugly like you so that her father may not know her again.' And 'place yourself upon her bosom,' whispered she to the third, 'that her heart may become corrupt and evil, a torment to herself.'

She then put the toads into the clear water, which was immediately tinted with a green colour, and having called Elise, took off her clothes and made her get into the bath – one toad settled among her hair, another on her forehead and the third upon her bosom; but Elise seemed not at all aware of it. She rose up, and three poppies were seen swimming on the water.

Had not the animals been poisonous and kissed by a witch, they would have been changed into roses while they remained on Elise's head and heart – she was too good for magic to have any power over her. When the queen realised this, she rubbed walnut juice all over the girl's skin, so that it became quite swarthy, smeared a nasty ointment over her lovely face, and entangled her long thick hair. It was impossible to recognise the beautiful Elise after this.

When her father saw her, he was shocked, and said she could not be his daughter; no-one would have anything to do with her but the mastiff and the swallows; but they, poor things, could not say anything in her favour.

Poor Elise wept, and thought of her eleven brothers, not one of whom she saw at the palace. In great distress she stole away and wandered the whole day over fields and moors, till she reached the forest. She knew not where to go, but she was so sad, and longed so much to see her brothers, who had been driven out into the world, that she determined to seek and find them.

She had not been long in the forest when night came on, and she lost her way amid the darkness. So she lay down on the soft moss, said her evening prayer, and leaned her head against the trunk of a tree. It was still in the forest, the air was mild, and from the grass and mould around gleamed the green light of many hundred glow-worms and when Elise lightly touched one of the branches hanging over her, bright insects fell down upon her like falling stars.

All night long she dreamed of her brothers. They were all children again, playing together, writing with diamond pens upon golden pads, and looking at the pictures in the beautiful book which had cost half a kingdom.

But they did not, as formerly, make straight strokes and question marks upon the pads; no they wrote of the bold actions they had performed, and the strange adventures they had encountered, and in the picture-book everything seemed alive. The birds sang, men and women stepped from the book and talked to Elise and her brothers. However, when she turned over the pages, they jumped back into their places, so that the pictures did not get confused together.

When Elise awoke the sun was already high in the sky. She could not see it clearly, for the tall trees of the forest entwined their thick-leaved branches closely together, and, as the sunbeams played upon them, they looked like a golden veil waving to and fro. The air was fragrant, and the birds perched upon Elise's shoulders. She heard the noise of water; there were several springs forming a pool, with the prettiest pebbles at the bottom; bushes were growing thickly round. But the deer had trodden a broad path through them, and by this path Elise went down to the water's edge. The water was so clear that, had not the boughs and bushes around been moved by the wind, you might have fancied they were painted upon the smooth surface, so distinctly was each little leaf mirrored upon it.

As soon as Elise saw her face reflected in the water, she was quite startled, so brown and ugly did it look; however, when she wetted her little hand, and rubbed her brow and eyes, the white skin again appeared. So Elise took off her clothes, stepped into the fresh water, and in the whole world there was not a king's daughter more beautiful than she then appeared.

After she dressed herself, and plaited her long hair, she went to the bubbling spring, drank out of the hollow of her hand, and then wandered farther into the forest. She did not know where she was going, but she thought of her brothers, and of the good God who, she felt, would never forsake her. It was He who made the wild crab-trees grow in order to feed the hungry, and who

showed her a tree whose boughs bent under the weight of their fruit. She made her noonday meal under its shade, propped against the boughs, and then walked on amid the dark twilight of the forest.

It was so still that she could hear her own footsteps, and the rustling of each little withered leaf that was crushed beneath her feet. Not a bird was to be seen; not a single sunbeam penetrated through the thick foliage; and the tall stems of the trees stood so close together, that when she looked straight before her, she seemed encircled by trellis-work. Oh! there was a loneliness in this forest such as Elise had never known before.

And the night was so dark! Not a single glow-worm sent forth its light. Depressed, she lay down to sleep and then it seemed to her as if the boughs above her opened, and she saw an angel looking down with a gentle face, and a thousand little cherubs all around him. When she awoke in the morning she could not tell whether this was a dream, or whether she had really been so watched.

She walked on and met an old woman with a basket full of berries; the old woman gave her some of them, and Elise asked if she had seen eleven princes ride through the wood.

'No,' said the old woman, 'but yesterday I saw eleven swans with golden crowns on their heads swim down the brook near this place.'

And she led Elise to a precipice, the base of which was washed by a brook; the trees on each side stretched their long leafy branches towards each other, and where they could not unite, the roots had disengaged themselves from the earth and hung over the water.

Elise bade the old woman farewell, and wandered by the side of the stream till she came to the place where it reached the open sea.

The beautiful sea lay stretched out before the girl's eyes, but not a ship, not a boat was to be seen; how was she to go on?

She observed the little stones on the shore, all of which the waves had washed into a round form; glass, iron, stone, everything that lay scattered there, had been moulded into shape, and yet the water which had done this was much softer than Elise's delicate little hand. 'It rolls on tirelessly,' she said, 'and softens what is so hard; I will be just as strong! Thank you for the lesson you have given me, bright rolling waves; some day, my heart tells me, you shall carry me to my dear brothers!'

There lay upon the wet seaweeds eleven white swan-feathers; Elise collected them together; drops of water hung about them, whether dew or tears she could not tell. She was quite alone on the seashore, but she did not mind that for the sea presented an eternal variety to her, more indeed in a few hours than the gentle inland waters would have offered in a whole year.

When a black cloud passed over the sky, it seemed as if the sea was saying, 'I too can look dark;' and then the wind would blow and the waves fling out their white foam. But when the clouds shone with a bright red tint, and the winds were asleep, the sea also became like a rose-leaf in hue. It was now green, now white; but as it rested peacefully, a slight breeze on the shore caused the water to heave gently like the bosom of a sleeping child.

At sunset Elise saw eleven wild swans with golden crowns on their heads flying towards the land; they flew one behind another, looking like a streaming white ribbon. Elise climbed the precipice, and concealed herself behind a bush; the swans settled close to her, and flapped their long white wings.

As the sun sank beneath the water, the swans also vanished, and in their place stood eleven handsome princes, the brothers of

Elise. She uttered a loud cry, for although they were very much altered, Elise knew them to be her brothers. She ran into their arms, called them by their names – and how happy *they* were to see and recognise their sister, who was now grown so tall and so beautiful! They laughed and wept, and soon told each other how wickedly their step-mother had treated them.

'We,' said the eldest of the brothers, 'fly or swim as long as the sun is above the horizon, but, when it sinks below, we appear again in our human form. We are therefore obliged to look out for a safe resting-place, for, if at sunset we were flying among the clouds, we should fall down as soon as we resumed our own form. We do not live here. A land quite as beautiful as this lies on the opposite side of the sea, but it is far off. To reach it, we have to cross the deep waters, and there is no island midway on which we may rest at night; one little solitary rock rises from the waves, and upon it we find only just room enough to stand side by side.

'There we spend the night in our human form, and when the sea is rough, we are sprinkled by its foam; but we are thankful for this resting-place, for without it we should never be able to visit our dear native country. Only once in the year is this visit to the home of our fathers permitted. We require two of the longest days for our flight, and can remain here only eleven days, during which time we fly over the large forest from where we can see the palace in which we were born, where our father lives, and the tower of the church in which our mother was buried.

'Here even the trees and bushes seem related to us; here the wild horses still race over the plains, as in the days of our childhood; here the charcoal burner still sings the same old tunes to which we used to dance in our youth; here we are still drawn, and here we have found you, dear little sister! We have two more days staying here; then we must fly over the sea to a land beautiful indeed, but not our fatherland. How shall we take you with us? We have neither ship nor boat!'

'How shall I be able to let you go?' said the sister. And so they went on talking almost the whole of the night. They slept for only a few hours.

Elise was awakened by the rustling of swans' wings which were fluttering above her. Her brothers were again transformed, and for some time flew around in large circles. At last they flew far, far away; one of them remained behind; it was the youngest, and he laid his head in her lap and she stroked his white wings. They remained the whole day together. Towards evening the others came back, and when the sun set, they stood again on the firm ground in their natural form.

'Tomorrow we shall fly away, and may not return for a year, but we cannot leave you; have you the courage to come with us? My arm is strong enough to bear you through the forest; shall we not have strength enough in our wings to carry you over the sea?'

'Yes, take me with you,' said Elise. They spent the whole night in weaving a mat of the pliant willow bark and the tough rushes, and their mat was thick and strong. Elise lay down upon it, and when the sun rose, and the brothers were again transformed into wild swans, they seized the mat with their beaks and flew up high among the clouds with their dear sister, who was still sleeping. The sunbeams shone full ·upon her face, so one of the swans flew over her head, and shaded her with his broad wings.

They were already far from land when Elise woke; she thought she was still dreaming, so strange did it appear to her to be travelling through the air, and over the sea. By her side lay a cluster of pretty berries, and a handful of delicious roots. Her youngest brother had laid them there; and she thanked him with a smile, for she knew him as the swan who flew over her head and shaded her with his wings.

They flew so high that the first ship they saw beneath them seemed like a white seagull hovering over the water. Elise saw behind her a large cloud, which looked like a mountain, and on it she saw the shadows of herself and the eleven swans. It formed a picture more splendid than any she had ever seen. But soon, however, the sun rose higher, the cloud remained far behind, and then the floating shadowy picture disappeared.

The whole day they continued to fly with a whizzing noise, like an arrow; but yet they went slower than usual – they had their sister to carry. A heavy tempest gathered as the evening approached; Elise anxiously watched the sun. It was setting; still the solitary rock could not be seen; it appeared to her that the swans flapped their wings with increasing vigour.

Alas! it would be her fault if her brothers did not arrive at the place in time! they would become human beings when the sun set, and if this happened before they reached the rocks, they would fall into the sea and be drowned. She prayed to God most fervently; still no rock was to be seen; the black clouds drew nearer, violent gusts of wind announced the approach of a storm, the clouds rested upon a huge wave which rolled quickly forwards, and one flash of lightning rapidly succeeded another.

The sun was now on the rim of the sea. Elise's heart beat violently; the swans shot downwards so swiftly that she thought she must fall. But again they began to hover; the sun was half sunk beneath the water, and at that moment she saw the little rock below her; it looked like a seal's head when he raises it just above the water. And the sun was sinking fast – it seemed scarcely larger than a star – her foot touched the hard ground, and the sun vanished like the last spark on a burnt piece of paper.

Arm in arm stood her brothers around her; there was only just room for her and them – the sea beat tempestuously against the rock, flinging over them a shower of foam. The sky seemed in a blaze, with the fast succeeding flashes of fire that lightened it, and peal after peal of thunder rolled on, but sister and brothers kept firm hold of each other's hands. They sang a hymn, and their hymn gave them comfort and courage.

By daybreak the air was pure and still, and, as soon as the sun rose, the swans flew away with Elise from the rock. The waves rose higher and higher, and when they looked from the clouds down upon the blackish-green sea, covered with white foam, they might have fancied that millions of swans were swimming on its surface.

As day advanced, Elise saw floating in the air before her a land of mountains with glaciers, and in the centre, a palace kilometres in length, with splendid colonnades, surrounded by palm-trees and gorgeous-looking flowers as large as mill-wheels. She asked if this was the country to which they were flying, but the swans shook their heads, for what she saw was the beautiful airy castle of the fairy Morgana, where no human being was admitted. Whilst Elise still bent her eyes upon it, mountains, trees, and castle all disappeared, and in their place stood twelve churches with high towers and pointed windows – she fancied she heard the organ play, but it was only the murmur of the sea. She was now close to these churches, but behold! they changed into a large fleet sailing under them; she looked down and saw it was only a sea-mist passing rapidly over the water. An endless variety floated before her eyes, till at last the land to which she was going appeared in sight. Beautiful blue mountains, cedar woods, towns and castles rose to view. Long before sunset Elise sat down among the mountains, in front of a large càvern; delicate young creepers grew thickly around, so that it appeared covered with gay embroidered carpets.

'Now we shall see what you will dream of tonight!' said her youngest brother, as he showed her the sleeping chamber destined for her.

'Oh, that I could dream how you might be freed from the spell!' she said; and this thought filled her mind. She prayed for God's help; even in her dreams she continued praying, and it appeared to her that she was flying up high in the air towards the castle of the fairy Morgana. The fairy came forward to meet her, radiant and beautiful, and yet she fancied she resembled the old woman who had given her berries in the forest, and told her of the swans with golden crowns.

'You can free your brothers,' said she; 'but have you courage and patience enough? The water is indeed softer than your delicate hands, and yet can mould the hard stones to its will, but then it cannot feel the pain which your tender fingers will feel; it has no heart and cannot suffer the anxiety and grief which you must suffer. Do you see these stinging-nettles which I have in my hand? There are many of the same kind growing round the cave where you are sleeping; only those that grow there or on the graves in the churchyard are of use, remember that!

'You must pluck them although they will sting your hand; you must trample on the nettles with your feet, and get yarn from them, and with this yarn you must weave eleven shirts with long sleeves; throw them over the eleven wild swans and the spell is broken. But remember this: from the moment you begin your work till it is completed, even should it take you years, you must not speak a word; the first syllable that escapes your lips will fall like a dagger into the hearts of your brothers; on your tongue depends their lives.'

And at the same moment the fairy touched Elise's hands with a nettle, which made them burn like fire, and Elise awoke. It was broad daylight, and close to her lay a nettle like the one she had seen in her dream. She fell upon her knees, thanked God, and then went out of the cave in order to begin her work. She plucked with her own delicate hands the stinging-nettles; they burned large blisters on her hands and arms, but she bore the pain willingly in the hope of releasing her dear brothers. She trampled on the nettles with her naked feet, and spun the green yarn.

At sunset her brothers came. Elise's silence quite frightened them; they thought it must be the effect of some fresh spell of their wicked stepmother. But when they saw her blistered hands, they realised what their sister was doing for their sakes. The youngest brother wept, and, when his tears fell upon her hands, Elise felt no more pain, and the blisters disappeared.

The whole night she spent in her work, for she could not rest till she had released her brothers. All the following day she sat in her solitude, for the swans had flown away, but never had time passed so quickly. One shirt was ready; she now began the second.

Suddenly a hunting horn resounded among the mountains. Elise was frightened. The noise came nearer; she heard the hounds barking; in great terror she fled into the cave, bound up the nettles which she had gathered and combed into a bundle, and sat down upon it.

In the same moment a large dog sprang out from the bushes. Two others immediately followed; they barked loudly, ran away, and then returned. It was not long before the hunters stood in front of the cave; the handsomest among them was the king of that country; he stepped up to Elise. Never had he seen a lovelier maiden.

'How did you come here, you beautiful girl?' he said.

Elise shook her head; she dared not speak, for a word might

have cost her the life of her brothers, and she hid her hands under
her apron in case the king should see how she was suffering.

'Come with me,' said he, 'you must not stay here! If you are as
good as you are beautiful, I will dress you in velvet and silk, I
will put a gold crown upon your head, and you shall live in
my palace!' So he lifted her upon his horse, while she wept and
wrung her hands; but the king said, 'I only desire your happiness!
you shall thank me for this some day!' and away he rode over
mountains and valleys, holding her on his horse in front, while the
other hunters followed.

When the sun set, the king's magnificent capital with its churches and domes lay before them, and the king led Elise into the palace, where, in a marble hall, fountains were playing, and the walls and ceilings displayed the most beautiful paintings. But Elise did not care for this splendour; she wept and mourned in silence, even while some female attendants dressed her in royal robes, wove costly pearls in her hair, and drew soft gloves over her blistered hands.

And now she was fully dressed, and, as she stood in her splendid attire, her beauty was so dazzling that the courtiers all bowed low before her, and the king chose her for his bride, although the archbishop shook his head, and whispered that the 'beautiful lady of the wood must certainly be a witch, who had blinded their eyes, and infatuated the king's heart.'

But the king did not listen; he ordered that music should be played. A sumptuous banquet was served up, and the loveliest maidens danced round the bride; she was led through fragrant gardens into magnificent halls, but not a smile was seen to play upon her lips, or beam from her eyes. The king then opened a small room next to her sleeping apartment; it was adorned with costly green tapestry, and exactly resembled the cave in which she had been found; upon the ground lay the bundle of yarn which she had spun from the nettles, and on the wall hung the shirt she had completed. One of the hunters had brought all this, thinking there must be something wonderful in it.

'Here you may dream of your former home,' said the king; 'here is the work which employed you; amidst all your present splendour it may sometimes give you pleasure to fancy yourself there again.'

When Elise saw what was so dear to her heart, she smiled, and the blood returned to her cheeks; she thought her brothers might still be freed, and she kissed the king's hand. He embraced her and ordered the bells of all the churches in the city to be rung, to announce the celebration of their wedding. The beautiful dumb maiden of the wood was to become queen of the land.

The archbishop whispered evil words in the king's ear, but they made no impression upon him; the marriage was solemnised, and the archbishop himself was obliged to put the crown upon her head. In his rage he pressed the narrow rim so firmly on her forehead that it hurt her, but a heavier weight – sorrow for her brothers – lay upon her heart, and she did not feel bodily pain. She was still silent, a single word would have killed her brothers; her eyes, however, beamed with heartfelt love to the king, so good and handsome, who had done so much to make her happy.

She became more warmly attached to him every day. Oh! how much she wished she might confide to him all her sorrows. But she was forced to remain silent; she could not speak until her work was completed. To this end she stole away every night, and went into the little room that was fitted up in imitation of the cave; there she worked at her shirts, but by the time she had begun the seventh, all her yarn was used up.

She knew that the nettles she needed grew in the churchyard, but she must gather them herself; how was she to get them?

'Oh, what is the pain in my fingers compared to the anguish my heart suffers!' she thought. 'I must venture to the churchyard; the good God will protect me!'

Fearful, as though she were about to do something wrong, one moonlight night she crept down to the garden, and through the long avenues into the lonely road leading to the churchyard. She saw sitting on one of the broadest tombstones a number of ugly old witches.

Elise was obliged to pass close by them, and the witches fixed their wicked eyes upon her; but she repeated her prayer, gathered the stinging-nettles, and took them back with her into the palace.

One person only had seen her; it was the archbishop, who was awake when others slept. Now he was convinced that all was not right about the queen: she must be a witch, who had, through her enchantments, infatuated the king and all the people.

Privately, he told the handsome king what he had seen, and what he feared; and, when the words came from his lips, the images of the saints shook their heads as though they would say, 'It is untrue; Elise is innocent!' But the archbishop explained the omen otherwise; he thought it was a testimony against her that the holy images shook their heads at hearing of her sin.

Two large tears rolled down the king's cheeks; he returned home in doubt; he pretended to sleep at night, though sleep never came to him and he noticed that Elise rose from her bed every night, and every time he secretly followed her and saw her enter her little room.

His countenance became darker every day; Elise noticed it, though she knew not the cause. She was much pained, and besides, what did she not suffer in her heart for her brothers! Her bitter tears ran down on the royal velvet and purple; they looked like bright diamonds, and all who saw the magnificence that surrounded her, wished themselves in her place.

She had now nearly finished her work, only one shirt was to be done; unfortunately, she needed more yarn also; she had not a single nettle left. Once more, only this one time, she must go to the churchyard and gather a few handfuls. She shuddered when she thought of the solitary walk and of the horrid witches, but her resolution was as firm as her trust in God.

Elise went, the king and archbishop followed her; they saw her disappear at the churchyard door, and, when they came nearer, they saw the witches sitting on the tombstone as Elise had seen them, and the king turned away, for he believed her whose head had rested on his bosom that very evening to be amongst them. 'Let the people judge her!' said he. And the people condemned her to be burned.

She was now dragged from the king's apartments into a dark damp prison, where the wind whistled through the barred window. Instead of velvet and silk, they gave her the bundle of nettles she had gathered; on that she must lay her head, and the shirts she had woven must serve her as mattress and counterpane.

But they could not have given her anything she valued so much; and she continued her work, at the same time praying earnestly to her God. The boys sang scandalous songs about her in front of her prison; not a soul comforted her with one word of love.

Towards evening she heard the rustling of swans' wings at the grating. It was the youngest of her brothers who had at last found his sister, and she sobbed aloud for joy, although she knew that the coming night would probably be the last of her life; but then her work was almost finished, and her brother was near.

The archbishop came in order to spend the last hour with her; he had promised the king he would; but she shook her head, and entreated him with her eyes and gestures to go. This night she must finish her work, or all she had suffered – her pain, her anxiety, her sleepless nights – would be in vain. The archbishop went away with many angry words, but the unfortunate Elise knew herself to be innocent, and went on with her work.

Little mice ran busily about and dragged the nettles to her feet wishing to help her; and the thrush perched on the iron bars of the window, and sang all night as merrily as he could, that Elise might not lose courage.

It was still darkness, just one hour before sunrise, when the eleven brothers stood before the palace gates, requesting an audience with the king. But it could not be, they were told; it was still night, the king was asleep, and they dared not wake him. They entreated, they threatened; the guard came up, and the king himself at last stepped out to ask what was the matter. At that moment the sun rose, the brothers could be seen no longer, and eleven white swans flew away over the palace.

The people poured forth from the gates of the city; they wished to see the witch burned. One sad old horse drew the cart in which Elise was placed. A coarse frock of sackcloth had been put on her, her beautiful long hair hung loosely over her shoulders, her cheeks were of a deadly paleness, her lips moved gently, and her fingers wove the green yarn. Even on her way to her cruel death she did not give up her work; the ten shirts lay at her feet, and she was now labouring to complete the eleventh. The rabble insulted her.

'Look at the witch, how she mutters! She has not a hymn-book in her hand; no, there she sits with her accursed black magic. Tear it from her; tear it into a thousand pieces!'

And they all crowded about her, and were on the point of snatching away the shirts, when eleven white swans came flying towards the cart; they settled all round her, and flapped their wings. The crowd gave way in terror.

'It is a sign from heaven! She is certainly innocent!' whispered some; they dared not say so aloud.

The sheriff now seized her by the hand; in a moment she threw the eleven shirts over the swans, and eleven handsome princes appeared in their place. The youngest had, however, only one

arm, and a wing instead of the other, for one sleeve was missing from his shirt – it had not been quite finished.

'Now I may speak,' said Elise: 'I am innocent!'

And the people who had seen what had happened bowed before her as before a saint. She, however, sank lifeless in her brothers' arms; suspense, fear and grief had quite exhausted her.

'Yes, she is innocent,' said her eldest brother, and he now related their wonderful history. Whilst he spoke a fragrance as delicious as though it came from millions of flowers spread itself around, for every piece of wood in the funeral pile had taken root and sent

forth branches. A hedge of blooming red roses surrounded
Elise, and above all the others blossomed a flower of dazzling
white colour, bright as a star. The king plucked it and laid it on
Elise's bosom, whereupon she awoke from her trance with peace
and joy in her heart.

And all the church-bells began to ring of their own accord; and
birds flew to the spot in swarms; and there was a festive procession
back to the palace, such as no king has ever seen equalled.

Three Aesop's Fables

The Lazy Tortoise

WHEN the great god Jupiter was married he gave a huge feast to which all living creatures were invited. They all arrived early except the tortoise, who came dawdling along at the end of the feast.

Jupiter was very angry. 'Why are you so late?' he demanded.

'I did not want to leave my home,' said the tortoise. 'I was quite content and happy there.'

Jupiter was angrier than ever to think that his guest preferred a ditch to a splendid palace. 'Very well,' said he, 'if you are so fond of your home, you will never again move around without carrying it on your back.'

And to this day, the tortoise still carries its house on its back.

Laziness finds its own punishment.

The Miser's Gold

A VERY mean man once sold all his estate and melted the money he received for it into one solid mass of gold. This he buried in the ground in his garden, and visited his hoard night and morning to gloat over it.

One night a robber spied on him and when the miser had gone back home dug up the treasure and went off with it. Next day the miser missed it and went nearly out of his mind at the loss of his gold. 'Why are you making such a noise?' said a neighbour. 'You might as well have a stone in the ground instead of your gold, for it was no use to you when you had it.'

Riches are meant to be used.

53

The Miller, his Son & the Ass

A MILLER and his son were driving their ass to a neighbouring fair to sell him.

They had not gone far when they met a troop of girls returning from the town, talking and laughing.

'Look there!' cried one of them; 'did you ever see such fools, to be trudging along the road on foot, when they might be riding!'

The old man, hearing this, quietly bade his son get on the ass, and walked along merrily by the side of him. Presently they came to a group of old men, who were talking together.

'There!' said one of them, 'it proves what I was saying. What respect is shown to old age in these days? Do you see that idle young rogue riding while his old father has to walk?'

'Get down, you good-for-nothing, and let the old man rest his weary limbs!' cried another.

Upon this the father made his son dismount and got up himself; but they had not proceeded far when they met a company of women and children.

'Why, you lazy old fellow!' cried several people at once, 'how can you ride upon the beast while this poor little lad can hardly keep pace by the side of you?'

The good-natured miller immediately took up his son behind him, and they rode in this manner until they had almost reached the town.

'Pray, honest friend,' said a townsman, 'is that ass your own?'

'Yes,' replied the old man.

'By the way you load him, one would not have thought so,' said the other. 'Why, you two fellows are better able to carry the poor beast than he you!'

'If you think it the right thing to do,' said the old man, 'we can but try.'

So, alighting with his son, they tied the ass's legs to a stout pole, which they shouldered, and so got ready to carry him over a bridge that led to the town.

This was so entertaining a sight that the people ran out in crowds to laugh at it, until the ass, not liking the noise nor the

situation, broke from the cords that bound him and tumbled off
the pole into the river below.

Annoyed and ashamed, the old man made his way home again,
convinced that by endeavouring to please everybody he had
pleased nobody, and lost his ass into the bargain.

He who tries to please everybody pleases nobody.

The Fairy Cobbler

THIS is the story that granny told me, sitting in her garden one summer evening, when I was sure I had just seen a fairy among the beans. Do I believe in fairies? Why, of course I do. Haven't I seen one with my own eyes. Seeing is believing, you know, and although this was many, many years ago, I can still tell you what the little fellow was like.

One day, I was sitting in the garden here, with my knitting in my hand. It was a fine, sunny day, about the middle of June. The bees were humming among the flowers; the birds were chirping and hopping on the bushes, and everything smelt fresh.

All of a sudden I heard among the rows of beans a noise that went tick-tack, tick-tack; it was just like a cobbler putting on the heel of a shoe.

'What can that be?' I said to myself.

So I laid down my knitting and went quietly over to the beans, and what do you think I saw? A little old man no bigger than my thumb, with such a funny little hat on his head! He had a little red coat on his back, and silver buckles on his shoes. Of course, I knew at once the little man was a fairy cobbler. You didn't think that the fairies needed shoemakers?

Oh, but they do, for the little people are so fond of dancing that they soon wear out their shoes. The fairy cobbler is the only fairy who works really hard. All the others do nothing but dance and play tricks.

The cobbler always carries a purse with a bright piece of silver in it. It is a great find to get your hands on a fairy purse.

Well, I kept as still as a cat when she is watching a mouse-hole. I could hear the tip-tap of the little fellow's hammer.

The fairy was laughing, too, all the time, as happy as a lark on an April morning. He had his back turned towards me, and was bending over the tiniest shoe I had ever seen.

Here was my chance to get a real fairy purse, I thought.

'That's hard work you're doing on this hot day,' I said to him.

The fairy turned swiftly round, and looked up at my face with a frightened look. I thought he was going to run away, so I caught hold of him.

'Where is your purse of money?' I asked.

'Money?' cried he; 'Money, indeed! And where would a poor little man like me get money?'

'Come, come,' I said, 'none of your tricks. Every one knows that the fairy cobblers always have money.'

I gave him a bit of a shake, and the little man looked so frightened that I almost pitied him.

'Come with me to the meadow,' said he, 'and I will show you where I keep my money.'

So I went to the meadow, still holding him in my hand, and keeping my eyes fixed upon him. If you take your eyes off a fairy for one moment, the little fellow can run away. All of a sudden I heard a loud *buzz* behind me.

'There! there!' cried the little man, 'your bees are all swarming and going off by themselves.'

Without thinking, I turned my head, but could see nothing. Then I looked angrily at the fairy, but, would you believe it? there was nothing in my hand. The moment I had looked round, he had slipped away, and he never came near my garden again.

The Dog in the Manger

A DOG once made his bed in a manger, and lay snarling and growling to keep the horses away from their food.
'What a miserable cur he is!' said one of the animals. 'He cannot eat the corn himself, nor will he let us eat it who are hungry.'

Live and let live.

The Fox & the Stork

A FOX one day invited a stork to dinner, and amused himself at the expense of his guest, by providing nothing for him to eat but some thin soup in a shallow dish.

This the fox lapped up very quickly, while the stork, unable to gain a mouthful with her long, narrow bill, was as hungry at the end of the dinner as when she began.

The fox expressed his regret at seeing her eat so sparingly, and feared that the dish was not seasoned to her liking.

The stork said but little, but begged that the fox would do her the honour of returning the visit next day, which invitation Reynard the fox readily accepted.

The fox kept the appointment, and, having greeted his hostess, turned his attention to the dinner placed before them.

To his dismay Reynard saw that the meal was served in a narrow-necked vessel, and, while the stork was able to thrust in her long bill and take her fill, he was obliged to content himself with licking the outside of the jar.

Unable to satisfy his hunger, he retired with as good grace as he could, knowing that he could hardly find fault with his hostess, for she had only paid him back in his own coin.

Those who love practical jokes must be prepared to laugh at themselves.

Beddgelert

BEDDGELERT lies near Snowdon in the county of Gwynedd, about 12 kilometres inland from the sea. 'Bedd' is the Welsh word for 'grave,' so Beddgelert means the 'Grave of Gelert.'

This is the story of how it came to be so called.

Many years ago there lived a brave chieftain, called Llewellyn, in Snowdonia. Now Llewellyn had a faithful dog, Gelert which had been presented to him by King John of England, and this dog was the leader of all Llewellyn's pack. At home he was as gentle as a lamb but in the hunt he was fierce and brave.

One day when Llewellyn and his men had assembled on the mountainside ready for hunting the hare, the huntsman blew a loud blast on his horn to rally the pack of hounds. To the huntsman's surprise, Gelert, the leader of the pack, was not there. So he blew again upon his horn. Still Gelert did not come. 'It seems very strange that Gelert does not come in answer to my call,' said the huntsman.

But they could not wait for him any longer and the huntsmen and the rest of the pack went on without him.

But somehow or other things went wrong that day. The chase was poor and the hound failed to run their quarry to earth.

At twilight Llewellyn rode sadly towards his castle. He was wondering greatly where Gelert had been all day. Just then he heard the familiar sound of his barking.

'Ah! Bad dog! Why did you fail me to-day? Where have you been?' Llewellyn began. But as he rode nearer he could see that something was wrong.

The dog did not bound forward to greet him as he usually did. He crouched low and licked his lips. Then, looking more closely at him, Llewellyn perceived that Gelert's coat was tangled and matted with clots of blood.

'What is the matter? Where did all this blood come from?' cried his master.

Here, there and everywhere the ground was smeared with it. Llewellyn dismounted hastily and ran into the castle. Here there were signs everywhere of a struggle. Blood, freshly-spilled, lay

61

all over the floor. No servants were there to answer to his call. Gelert followed at his master's heels, dragging his hind legs somewhat.

Quickly Llewellyn's gaze travelled to the cradle in which he had left his baby son. He rushed up to it. The baby was not there! The coverlet was torn and smeared with blood. All was in disorder. Llewellyn had only one thought at the time. 'Cruel monster!' he cried to the dog. 'You have betrayed my trust and devoured my son!'

The poor dumb creature's eyes searched his master's face.

'If only I could speak!' he seemed to say. He crouched low and tried to lick his master's feet. But Llewellyn was furious.

'You, too, shall die, treacherous hound!' And so saying he plunged his sword into Gelert's side.

His dying yelp was heard from afar. It woke Llewellyn's sleeping child who murmured and cried out.

The chieftain searched in the direction from which the sound came. There, in another room, quite safe and sound, beneath a heap of bloodstained clothes, lay the child.

At his side, torn and mangled, but quite dead, lay an enormous wolf!

Now the truth was made clear to Llewellyn. The gallant dog had fought with the wolf and had killed him, in order to save the life of the child he so jealously guarded.

Llewellyn's grief was pitiful to behold. 'The desperate deed which laid you low, this heart shall ever regret,' said he.

So Gelert was buried with ceremony and there beneath a mound of stones, his grave can still be seen to this day.

Snow-White

IT was in the middle of winter, when the broad flakes of snow were falling around, that a certain queen sat working at a window, the frame of which was made of fine, black ebony, and as she was looking out upon the snow she pricked her finger and three drops of blood fell from it. Then she gazed thoughtfully upon the red drops which sprinkled the white snow, and said, 'Would that my little daughter may be as white as that snow, as red as the blood, and as black as the ebony window-frame.' And so the little girl grew up: her skin was as white as snow, her cheeks as rosy as the blood, and her hair as black as ebony, and she was called Snow-White.

But this queen died, and the king soon married another wife, who was very beautiful, but so proud that she could not bear to think that anyone could surpass her. She had a magical looking-glass, where she used to go and gaze upon herself and say:

> 'Tell me, glass, tell me true!
> Of all the ladies in the land,
> Who is the fairest? Tell me who?'

and the glass answered:

> 'Thou, Queen, art fairest in the land.'

But Snow-White grew more and more beautiful, and when she was seven years old she was as bright as the day and fairer

than the queen herself. Then the looking-glass one day answered the proud queen, when she went to consult it as usual:

> *'Thou, Queen, may'st fair and beauteous be,*
> *But Snow-White is lovelier far then thee!'*

When she heard this she turned pale with rage and envy, and called to one of her servants and said: 'Take Snow-White away into the wide wood that I may never see her again.' Then the servant led her away, but his heart melted when she begged him to spare her life, and he said, 'I will not hurt you, you pretty child.' So he left her by herself, and though he thought it most likely that the wild beasts would tear her to pieces, he felt as if a great weight were taken off his heart when he had made up his mind not to kill her but to leave her to her fate.

Then poor Snow-White wandered along through the wood in great fear, and the wild beasts roared about her, but none did her any harm. In the evening she came to a little cottage and went in there to rest herself, for her little feet would carry her no farther. Everything was spruce and neat in the cottage; on the table was spread a white cloth, and there were seven little plates with seven little loaves, and seven little glasses with wine in them, and knives and forks laid in order; and by the wall stood seven little beds. Then, as she was very hungry, she picked a little piece off

each loaf, and drank a very little wine out of each glass, and after that she thought she would lie down and rest. So she tried all the little beds, and one was too long, and another was too short, till at last the seventh suited her and there she laid herself down and went to sleep.

Presently in came the masters of the cottage, who were seven little dwarfs that lived among the mountains, and dug and searched about for gold. They lighted up their seven lamps and

saw directly that all was not right. The first said, 'who has been sitting on my stool?' The second, 'who has been eating off my plate?' The third 'who has been picking my bread?' The fourth, 'who has been meddling with my spoon?' The fifth, 'who has been handling my fork?' The sixth, 'who has been cutting with my knife?' The seventh, 'who has been drinking my wine?' Then the first looked round and said, 'who has been lying on my bed?' And the rest came running to him, and everyone cried out that somebody had been upon his bed. But the seventh saw Snow-White, and called all his brothers to come and see her, and they cried out with wonder and astonishment and brought their lamps to look at her, and said: 'Good heavens, what a lovely child she is.' And they were delighted to see her and took care not to wake her, and the seventh dwarf slept an hour with each of the other dwarfs in turn, till the night was gone.

In the morning, Snow-White told them all her story and they pitied her and said if she would keep all things in order, and cook and wash, and knit and spin for them, she might stay where she was and they would take good care of her. Then they went out all day long to their work, seeking for gold and silver in the mountains, and Snow-White remained at home, and they warned her and said: 'The queen will soon find out where you are, so take care and let no one in.'

But the queen, now that she thought Snow-White was dead, believed that she was certainly the handsomest lady in the land and she went to her glass and said:

'Tell me, glass, tell me true!
Of all the ladies in the land,
Who is the fairest? Tell me who?'

And the glass answered:

'Thou, queen, art the fairest in all this land;
But over the hills, in the greenwood shade,
Where the seven dwarfs their dwelling have made,
There Snow-White is hiding her head, and she
Is lovelier far, O queen, than thee!'

Then the queen was very much alarmed, for she knew that the glass always spoke the truth, and was sure that the servant had betrayed her. And she could not bear to think that anyone lived who was more beautiful than she was, so she disguised herself as an old pedlar and went her way over the hills to the place where the dwarfs lived.

Then she knocked at the door and cried, 'fine wares to sell!'

Snow-White looked out of the window and said, 'Good day, good woman, what have you to sell?'

'Good wares, fine wares,' she said, 'silks and cottons of all colours.'

'I will let the old lady in, she seems to be a very good sort of person,' thought Snow-White, so she ran down and unbolted the door.

'Bless me,' said the old woman, 'your belt is undone. Let me do it up for you.' Snow-White did not dream of any mischief, so she stood up before the old woman, who set to work nimbly and pulled the belt so tight that Snow-White lost her breath and fell down as if she were dead. 'There's an end of all your beauty,' said the spiteful queen, and went away home.

In the evening the seven dwarfs returned, and were so grieved to see their faithful Snow-White stretched upon the ground motionless as if she were quite dead. However, they lifted her up and when they found what was the matter, they cut the belt and in a little time she began to breathe and soon came to life again. Then they said: 'The old woman was the queen herself, take care

another time and let no one in when we are away.'

When the queen got home she went straight to her glass and spoke to it as usual, but to her surprise it still said:

> '*Thou, queen, art the fairest in all this land;*
> *But over the hills, in the greenwood shade,*
> *Where the seven dwarfs their dwelling have made,*
> *There Snow-White is hiding her head, and she*
> *Is lovelier far, O queen, than thee!*'

Then the blood ran cold in her heart with spite and malice to see that Snow-White still lived, and she dressed herself up again in a disguise, but very different from the one she wore before, and took with her a poisoned comb. When she reached the dwarfs' cottage she knocked at the door and cried, 'fine wares to sell!' But Snow-White said, 'I dare not let anyone in.' Then the queen said, 'only look at my beautiful combs,' and gave her the poisoned one. And it looked so pretty that she took it up and put it into her hair to try it, but the moment it touched her head the poison was so powerful that she fell down senseless. 'There you may lie,' said the queen, and went her way. But by good luck the dwarfs returned very early that evening, and when they saw Snow-White lying on the ground they thought what had happened, and soon found the poisoned comb. And when they took it away, she recovered and told them all that had passed, and they warned her once more not to open the door to anyone.

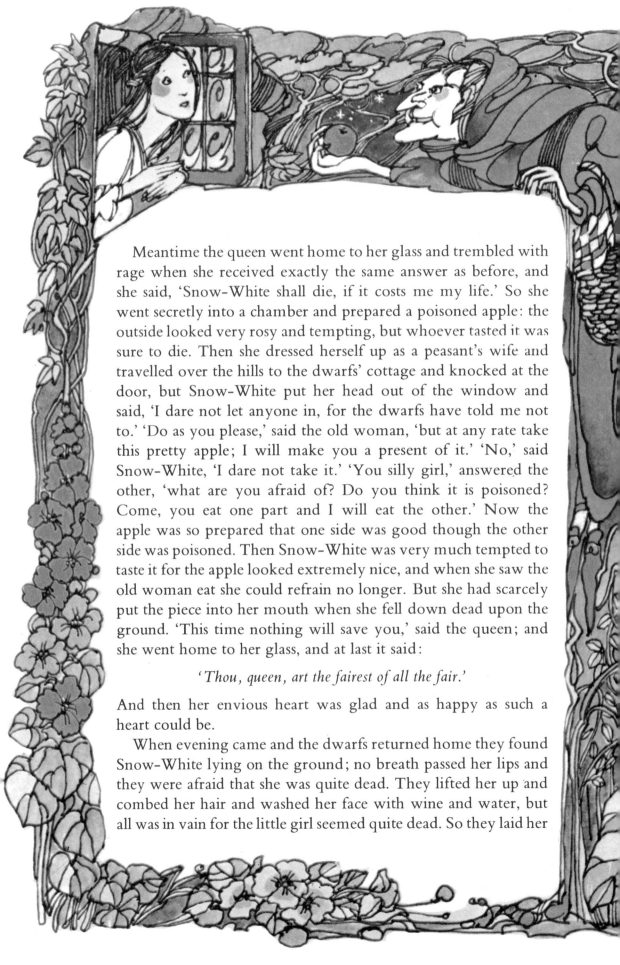

Meantime the queen went home to her glass and trembled with
rage when she received exactly the same answer as before, and
she said, 'Snow-White shall die, if it costs me my life.' So she
went secretly into a chamber and prepared a poisoned apple: the
outside looked very rosy and tempting, but whoever tasted it was
sure to die. Then she dressed herself up as a peasant's wife and
travelled over the hills to the dwarfs' cottage and knocked at the
door, but Snow-White put her head out of the window and
said, 'I dare not let anyone in, for the dwarfs have told me not
to.' 'Do as you please,' said the old woman, 'but at any rate take
this pretty apple; I will make you a present of it.' 'No,' said
Snow-White, 'I dare not take it.' 'You silly girl,' answered the
other, 'what are you afraid of? Do you think it is poisoned?
Come, you eat one part and I will eat the other.' Now the
apple was so prepared that one side was good though the other
side was poisoned. Then Snow-White was very much tempted to
taste it for the apple looked extremely nice, and when she saw the
old woman eat she could refrain no longer. But she had scarcely
put the piece into her mouth when she fell down dead upon the
ground. 'This time nothing will save you,' said the queen; and
she went home to her glass, and at last it said:

'*Thou, queen, art the fairest of all the fair.*'

And then her envious heart was glad and as happy as such a
heart could be.

When evening came and the dwarfs returned home they found
Snow-White lying on the ground; no breath passed her lips and
they were afraid that she was quite dead. They lifted her up and
combed her hair and washed her face with wine and water, but
all was in vain for the little girl seemed quite dead. So they laid her

down upon a bier and all seven watched and bewailed her for
three whole days, and then they proposed to bury her, but her
cheeks were still rosy and her face looked just as it did while she
was alive, so they said, 'We will never bury her in the cold
ground.' And they made a coffin of glass so that they might still
look at her, and wrote her name upon it in golden letters, and
that she was a king's daughter. And the coffin was placed upon
the hill and one of the dwarfs always sat by it and watched. And
the birds of the air came too, and mourned Snow-White: first
of all came a wise owl, and then a coal-black raven, but at last
came a gentle dove.

And thus Snow-White lay for a long, long time, and still only
looked as though she were asleep, for she was even now as white
as snow, and as red as blood, and as black as ebony. At last a
prince came and called at the dwarfs' house, and he saw Snow-
White and read what was written in golden letters. Then he
offered the dwarfs money and earnestly prayed them to let him
take her away, but they said: 'We will not part with her for all
the gold in the world.' At last, however, they had pity on him
and gave him the coffin: but the moment he lifted it up to carry it
home with him, the piece of apple fell from between her lips and
Snow-White awoke and said, 'Where am I?' And the prince
answered, 'You are safe with me.' Then he told her all that had
happened and said, 'I love you better than all the world, come
with me to my father's palace and you shall be my wife.' And
Snow-White consented and went home with the prince, and
everything was prepared with great pomp and splendour for
their wedding.

To the feast was invited, among the rest, Snow-White's old enemy, the queen; and as she was dressing herself in fine, rich clothes, she looked in the glass and said:

> *'Tell me, glass, tell me true!*
> *Of all the ladies in the land,*
> *Who is the fairest? Tell me who?'*

And the glass answered:

> *'Thou, lady, art loveliest* here, *I ween;*
> *But lovelier far is the new-made Queen.'*

When she heard this, she started with rage, but her envy and curiosity were so great that she could not help setting out to see the bride. And when she arrived and saw that it was none other than Snow-White who, as she thought, had been dead a long while, she choked with rage and fell ill and died. But Snow-White and the prince lived and reigned happily over that land for many, many years.

The Mice Meeting

ONCE upon a time a number of mice called a meeting to decide upon the best means of ridding themselves of a cat that had killed many of their relations.

Various plans were discussed and rejected, until at last a young mouse proposed that a bell should be hung round the tyrant's neck, in future, so that they would have warning of her movements and be able to escape.

The suggestion was received joyfully by nearly all, but an old mouse, who had sat silent for some time, got up and said: 'While I consider the plan to be a very clever one, and feel sure that it would prove to be quite successful if carried out, I should like to know who is going to put a bell on the cat?'

It is easier to make a suggestion than to carry it out.

The Town Mouse & the Country Mouse

ONCE upon a time a country mouse who had a friend in town invited him to pay him a visit in the country.

The invitation being duly accepted, the country mouse, though plain and rough in his habits of living, opened his heart in honour of an old friend. There was not a carefully stored-up morsel that he did not bring forth out of his larder – peas and barley, cheese-parings and nuts – hoping by quantity to make up what he feared was lacking in quality.

The town mouse, who was used to more dainty food, at first picked a bit here and a bit there, while the host sat nibbling a blade of barley straw.

At length he exclaimed, 'How is it, my good friend, that you can endure the dullness of this life? You are living like a toad in a hole. You can't really prefer these lonely rocks and woods to streets filled with shops and carriages and men! Believe me, you are wasting your time here. We must make the most of life while it lasts. A mouse, you know, does not live for ever. So come with me, and I'll show you life and the town.'

These fine words were too much for the simple country mouse, and he agreed to go with his friend to town.

It was late in the evening when the two crept into the city, and midnight before they reached the great house where the town mouse lived. Here were couches of crimson velvet, carvings in ivory, everything, in fact, that showed wealth and comfort. On the table were the remains of a splendid meal, and it was now the turn of the town mouse to play the host; he ran to and fro to supply his friend's wants, pressed dish upon dish and titbit upon titbit, as though he were waiting on a king.

The country mouse, for his part, tried to appear quite at home, and blessed the good fortune that had brought such a change in his way of life; when, in the midst of his enjoyment, as he was wondering how he could have been content with the poor food he was used to at home, suddenly the door opened and a party of ladies and gentlemen entered the room.

The two friends jumped from the table in the greatest fright, and hid themselves in the first corner they could reach. When the room was quiet again they ventured to creep out, but the barking of dogs drove them back in still greater terror than before.

At length, when all the household was asleep, the country mouse stole out from his hiding-place, and, bidding his host good-bye, whispered in his ear, 'My good friend, this fine mode of living may do for those who like it, but give me barley and bread in peace and security before the tastiest feast where fear and care lie in wait.'

*A humble life with peace and quiet
is better than a splendid one with danger and risk.*

The Fox & the Goat

ONE day a fox fell into a well, and wondered how he could get out again. At last a goat came along, and, feeling thirsty, he asked Reynard if the water was good.

The fox saw his chance, and, pretending that he was swimming for pleasure, replied, 'Yes come down, my friend; the water is so nice that I cannot drink enough of it, and there is plenty for both of us.' So the goat jumped in, and the artful fox, making use of his friend's horns, quickly sprang out.

When he was safely on top of the well, he coolly remarked to the poor goat, 'Had you half as much brains as you have beard, you would have looked before you leaped.'

Think before you act.

The Bees, the Drones & the Wasps

S OME bees built a comb in the hollow trunk of an oak-tree, but some drones claimed that they had built it, and that it belonged to them.

The case was brought into court before Judge Wasp, who, knowing the habits of both parties, addressed them thus:

'The plaintiffs and defendants are so much alike in shape and colour that it is difficult to say which are the rightful owners, and the case has very properly been brought before me. Now I think that justice will best be served now by following the plan which I propose. Let each party take a hive and build up a new comb, so that from the shape of the cells and the taste of the honey it will be quite clear to whom the comb in dispute belongs.'

The bees readily agreed to the wasp's plan, but the drones, on the other hand, would not do so.

Whereupon the wasp gave judgment: 'It is clear now who made the comb, and who cannot make it; the court gives judgment in favour of the bees.'

We may know a tree by its fruit.

The Fox & the Lion

WHEN a fox who had never seen a lion met one for the first time he was so terrified that he almost died of fright. When he met him the second time, however, he was still afraid, but managed to hide his fear. But when he saw him for the third time he felt so brave that he went up and began to talk to him as though they were old friends.

Familiarity breeds contempt.

The Charger & the Ass

A CHARGER, beautifully groomed and equipped, one day came galloping along a road, exciting the envy of a poor ass who was trudging along with a heavy load.

'Get out of my way!' cried the proud horse, 'or I shall trample you under my feet.'

The ass said nothing, but quietly moved to one side of the road.

Not long afterwards the charger went to the wars, and was badly wounded on the battlefield. Unfit for any further military service, he was sent home to work on the farm.

The ass saw him there painfully dragging a heavy wagon. 'Ah!' said he to himself, 'I need not have envied him in his pride; but for that he would have a true friend to help him in his need and lighten his load.'

He who despises a humble friend may be doing an ill turn to himself.

Rapunzel

ONCE upon a time there lived a man and his wife who very much wished to have a child, but for a long time in vain. Finally, the wife became pregnant. These people had a little window in the back part of their house, out of which they could see a beautiful garden, which was full of fine flowers and vegetables; but it was surrounded by a high wall, and no one dared to go in, because it belonged to a witch, who possessed great power, and who was feared by the whole world.

One day the woman stood at this window looking into the garden, and there she saw a bed which was filled with the most beautiful radishes, and which seemed so fresh and green that she felt quite glad, and a great desire to eat them seized her. This wish tormented her daily, and as she knew that she could not have them, she fell ill, and looked very pale and miserable. This frightened her husband, who asked her, 'What is the matter, my dear wife?'

'Ah!' she replied, 'if I cannot get any of those radishes to eat out of the garden behind the house, I shall die!'

Her husband, loving her very much, thought, 'rather than let my wife die, I must fetch her some radishes, whatever the cost.'

So, in the gloom of the evening, he climbed the wall of the witch's garden, and, snatching a handful of radishes in great haste, brought them to his wife, who made herself a salad with them, which she enjoyed very much. However, they were so nice and so well flavoured, that the next day after she felt the same desire for the third time, and could not get any rest, her husband was obliged to promise her some more.

So, in the evening, he made himself ready, and began clambering up the wall; but oh! how terribly frightened he was, for there he saw the old witch standing before him. 'How dare you,' she began, looking at him with a frightful scowl – 'how dare you climb over into my garden to take away my radishes like a thief? Evil shall happen to you for this.'

'Ah!' replied he, 'let pardon be granted before justice. I have only done this from a great necessity: my wife saw your radishes from her window, and took such a fancy to them that she would have died if she had not eaten them.' So then the witch ran after him in a fury, saying, 'If she behaves as you say, I will let you take away all the radishes you please; but I make one condition – you must give me your child. All shall go well with it, and I will care for it like a mother.'

In his anxiety the man consented, and when the child was born the witch appeared at the same time, gave the child the name 'Rapunzel,' and took it away with her.

Rapunzel grew to be the most beautiful child under the sun, and when she was twelve years old the witch shut her up in a tower, which stood in a forest, and had neither stairs nor door, and only one little window just at the top. When the witch wished to enter, she stood beneath, and called out:

> 'Rapunzel! Rapunzel!
> Let down your hair.'

For Rapunzel had long and beautiful hair, as fine as spun gold, and, as soon as she heard the witch's voice, she unbound her tresses, opened the window, and then the hair fell down and the witch climbed up by it.

After a couple of years had passed away, it happened that the king's son was riding through the wood, and came by the tower. There he heard a song so beautiful that he stood still and listened.

It was Rapunzel, who, to pass the time of her loneliness away, was exercising her sweet voice. The king's son wished to ascend to her, and looked for a door in the tower, but he could not find one.

So he rode home, but the song had touched his heart so much that he went every day to the forest and listened to it; and as he stood one day behind a tree, he saw the witch come up, and heard her call out:

> 'Rapunzel! Rapunzel!
> Let down your hair.'

Then Rapunzel let down her tresses, and the witch mounted up. Is that the ladder on which one must climb? Then I will try my

luck too,' said the prince; and the following day, as he felt quite
lonely, he went to the tower, and said:

> '*Rapunzel! Rapunzel!*
> *Let down your hair.*'

Then the tresses fell down, and he climbed up.

Rapunzel was very much frightened at first when a man
came in, for she had never seen one before; but the king's son
talked in a loving way to her, and told how his heart had been so
moved by her singing that he had no peace until he had seen her
himself.

So Rapunzel lost her terror, and when he asked her if she
would have him for a husband, and she saw that he was young
and handsome, she thought, 'I would like to marry him.' So,
saying 'Yes,' she put her hand within his. 'I will willingly go
with you, but I know not how I am to descend. When you come,
bring with you a skein of silk each time, out of which I will
weave a ladder, and when it is ready I will come down by it, and
you must take me upon your horse.'

Then they agreed that they should never meet till the evening,
as the witch came in the daytime. The old woman found out
nothing, until one day Rapunzel innocently said, 'Tell me,
madam, how it happens you find it more difficult to come up to
me than the king's young son, who climbs up in a moment!'

'Oh, you wicked child!' exclaimed the witch, 'what do I hear?
I thought I had separated you from all the world, and yet you
have deceived me.' And, seizing Rapunzel's beautiful hair in a
fury, she gave her a couple of blows with her left hand, and,

taking a pair of scissors in her right, *snip, snap*, she cut off all her beautiful tresses, and they fell upon the ground. Then she was so hard-hearted that she took the poor maiden into a great desert, and left her to die in great misery and grief.

But in the evening of the same day on which she had carried off Rapunzel, the old witch tied the shorn tresses so securely to the window-latch that when the king's son came, and called out:

'Rapunzel! Rapunzel!
Let down your hair.'

she let them down. The prince mounted, but when he got to the top he found, not his dear Rapunzel, but the witch, who looked at him with furious and wicked eyes.

'Aha!' she exclaimed scornfully, 'you would fetch your dear wife; but the beautiful bird sits no longer in her nest, singing; the cat has taken her away, and will now scratch out your eyes. To you Rapunzel is lost; you will never see her again.'

The prince lost his senses with grief at these words, and sprang out of the window of the tower in his bewilderment. He escaped with his life, but the thorns into which he fell put out his eyes. So he wandered, blind, in the forest, eating nothing but berries and roots, and doing nothing but weep and lament for the loss of his dear wife.

He wandered about in great misery, for some few years, and at last arrived at the desert where Rapunzel, who had given birth to

twins – a boy and girl – lived in great sorrow. Hearing a voice
which he thought he knew, he followed in its direction, and,
as he approached, Rapunzel recognised him, and fell into his
arms and wept. Two of her tears moistened his eyes, and they
became clear again, so that he could see as well as ever.

Then he led her away to his kingdom, where he was received
with great demonstrations of joy, and where they lived for a
long time, contented and happy.

What became of the old witch no one ever knew.

Hansel & Gretel

ONCE upon a time there lived near a large wood a poor
woodcutter, with his wife and two children by his
former marriage – a little boy called Hansel, and a girl
named Gretel. He had little enough to eat or drink and once,
when there was a great famine in the land, he could not procure
even his daily bread; and as he was sitting by the fire one evening,
restless and very troubled, he sighed, and said to his wife, 'What
will become of us? How can we feed our children when we have
not sufficient to eat ourselves?'

'Know then, my husband,' she answered, 'we will lead them
away quite early in the morning into the thickest part of the
wood, and there make them a fire, and give them each a little
piece of bread. Then we will go to our work and leave them
alone so they will not find their way home again, and we shall be
freed from them.'

'No wife,' replied he, 'that I can never do. How can you bring
yourself to leave my children all alone in the wood – for the
wild beasts will soon come and tear them to pieces.'

'Oh, you simpleton!' said she, 'then we must all four die of
hunger; you had better plane the coffins for us.' But she left him
no peace till he consented, saying, 'Ah, but I shall miss the poor
children.'

The two children, however, had not gone to sleep for hunger,
and so they overheard what the step-mother said to their father.

Gretel wept bitterly, and said to Hansel, 'what will become of us?' 'Be quiet, Gretel,' said he; 'do not cry – I will soon help you.' And as soon as their parents had fallen asleep, he got up, put on his coat, and, unbarring the back door, slipped out.

The moon shone brightly, and the white pebbles which lay before the door seemed like silver pieces, they glittered so brightly. Hansel stooped down and put as many into his pocket as it would hold; and then going back, he said to Gretel, 'Be comforted, dear sister, and sleep in peace; God will not forsake us'; and so saying, he went to bed again.

The next morning, before the sun arose, the wife went and awoke the two children. 'Get up, you lazy things; we are going into the forest to chop wood.' Then she gave them each a piece of bread, saying, 'there is something for your dinner; do not eat it before the time, for you will get nothing else.'

Gretel took the bread in her apron, for Hansel's pocket was full of pebbles, and so they all set out upon their way. When they had gone a little distance, Hansel stood still, and peeped back at the house; and this he repeated several times, till his father said, 'Hansel, what are you peeping at, and why do you lag behind? Take care, and watch your feet.'

'Ah, father,' said Hansel, 'I am looking at my white cat sitting upon the roof of the house, and trying to say goodbye.' 'You simpleton!' said the wife, 'that is not a cat; it is only the sun shining on the white chimney.' But in reality Hansel was not looking at a cat; but every time he stopped he dropped a pebble out of his pocket upon the path.

When they came to the middle of the wood, the father told the children to collect some sticks and he would make them a fire, so that they should not be cold; so Hansel and Gretel gathered together quite a little mountain of twigs. Then they set fire to them, and as the flame burned up high, the wife said, 'Now you children, lie down near the fire and rest yourselves, whilst we go into the forest and chop wood; when we are ready, I will come and call you.'

Hansel and Gretel sat down by the fire, and when it was noon, each ate the piece of bread; and because they could hear the blows of an axe, they thought their father was near; but it was not an axe, but a branch which he had bound to a withered tree, so as to be blown to and fro by the wind. They waited so long that at last their eyes closed from weariness, and they fell fast asleep.

When they awoke it was quite dark, and Gretel began to cry. 'How shall we get out of the wood?' But Hansel tried to comfort her by saying, 'wait a little while till the moon rises, and then we will quickly find the way.'

The moon shone forth, and Hansel, taking his sister's hand, followed the pebbles, which glittered like new-minted silver pieces, and showed them the path. All night long they walked on, and as day broke they came to their father's house. They knocked at the door, and when the wife opened it, and saw Hansel and Gretel, she exclaimed, 'You wicked children! why did you sleep so long in the wood? We thought you were never coming home again.' But their father was very glad, for it had made him bitterly sad to leave them all alone.

Not long afterwards there was again great scarcity in every corner of the land; and one night the children overheard their mother saying to their father, 'Everything is again eaten; we have only half a loaf left, and then everything is over; the children must be sent away. We will take them deeper into the wood, so that they may not find the way out again; it is the only means of escape for us.'

But her husband felt heavy at heart, and thought, 'it would be better to share the last crust with the children.' His wife, however, would listen to nothing that he said, and scolded and reproached him without stopping.

He who says A must say B too; and he who consents the first time must also the second.

The children, however, had again heard the conversation as they lay awake, and as soon as the old people went to sleep Hansel got up, intending to pick up some pebbles as before; but the wife had locked the door, so that he could not get out. Nevertheless he comforted Gretel, saying, 'Do not cry; sleep in peace; God will not forsake us.'

Early in the morning the step-mother came and pulled them out of bed, and gave them each a slice of bread, which was still smaller than the former piece. On the way, Hansel broke his in his pocket, and, stooping every now and then, dropped a crumb upon the path.

'Hansel, why do you stop and look about?' said the father; 'keep to the path.' 'I am looking at my little dove,' answered Hansel, 'nodding a good-bye to me.' 'Simpleton!' said the wife, 'that is no dove, but only the sun shining on the chimney.' But Hansel still kept dropping crumbs as he went along.

The mother led the children deep into the wood, where they had never been before, and there making an immense fire, she said to them, 'Sit down here and rest, and when you feel tired you can sleep for a little while. We are going into the forest to chop wood, and in the evening, when we are ready, we will come and fetch you.'

When noon came, Gretel shared her bread with Hansel, who had scattered his on the path. Then they went to sleep; but the evening arrived, and no one came to visit the poor children. In the dark night they awoke, and Hansel comforted his sister by saying, 'Only wait, Gretel, till the moon comes out, then we shall see the crumbs of bread which I have dropped, and they will show us the way home.'

The moon shone, and they got up, but they could not see any crumbs, for the thousands of birds which had been flying about in the woods and fields had picked them all up. Hansel kept saying to Gretel, 'we will soon find the way.' But they did not, and they walked the whole night long and the next day, but still they did not come out of the wood; and they got so hungry, for they had nothing to eat but some of the berries which they found upon the bushes. Soon they got so tired that they could not drag themselves along, so they lay down under a tree and went to sleep on a soft bed of ferns.

It was now the third morning since they had left their father's house, and they still walked on; but they only got deeper and deeper into the wood, and Hansel saw that if help did not come very soon they would die of hunger. As soon as it was noon they saw a beautiful snow-white bird sitting upon a bough, which sang so sweetly that they stood still and listened to it. It soon stopped and, spreading its wings, flew away; and they followed it until it arrived at a cottage, upon the roof of which it perched;

and when they went close up to it they saw that the cottage was made of bread and cakes, and the window-panes were made of clear sugar.

'We will go in there,' said Hansel, 'and have a glorious feast. I will eat a piece of the roof, and you can eat the window. Won't they be sweet?'

So Hansel reached up and broke a piece off the roof, in order to see how it tasted; while Gretel stepped up to the window and began to bite it.

Then a sweet voice called out in the room. 'Tip-tap, tip-tap, who raps at my door?' And the children answered: 'The wind, the wind, the child of heaven.' And they went on eating without interruption.

Hansel thought the roof tasted very nice, and so he tore off a great piece, while Gretel broke a large round pane out of the window, and sat down quite contentedly. Just then the door opened, and a very old woman, walking upon crutches, came out. Hansel and Gretel were so frightened that they let fall what they had in their hands, but the old woman, nodding her head,

said, 'Ah, you dear children, what has brought you here? Come in and stay with me, and no harm shall befall you.' And so saying, she took them both by the hand and led them into her cottage.

A good meal of milk and pancakes, with sugar, apples and nuts, was spread on the table, and in the back room were two nice little beds, covered with white, where Hansel and Gretel laid themselves down, and thought themselves in heaven. The old woman behaved very kindly to them, but in reality she was a wicked witch who waylaid children, and built the breadhouse in order to entice them in, and as soon as they were in her power she killed, cooked and ate them, and made a great festival of the day.

Witches have red eyes, and cannot see very far, but they have a fine sense of smell, like wild beasts, so that they know when children approach them. When Hansel and Gretel came near the witch's house she laughed wickedly, saying, 'here come two who shall not escape me.' And early in the morning, before they awoke, she went up to them, and saw how sweetly they lay sleeping, with their chubby red cheeks, and she mumbled to herself, 'that will be a good bite.'

Then she took up Hansel with her rough hand, and shut him up in a little cage with a lattice-door; and although he screamed loudly it was no use. Next she went to Gretel, and, shaking her till she awoke, said; 'Get up, you lazy thing, and fetch some water to cook something good for your brother, who must remain in that stall and get fat; when he is fat enough I shall eat him.'

'Gretel,' she called out in a rage, 'get some water quickly: made her do as she wished. So a nice meal was cooked for Hansel, but Gretel got nothing else but a crab's claw.

Every morning the old witch came to the cage, and said, 'Hansel, stretch out your finger that I may feel whether you are getting fat.' But Hansel used to stretch out a bone, and the old woman, having very bad sight, thought it was his finger, and wondered very much that he did not get fatter. When four weeks had passed, and Hansel still remained thin, she lost all her patience and would not wait any longer.

'Gretel,' she called out in a rage, 'get some water quickly: whether Hansel is fat or thin, today I will kill and cook him.'

Oh! how the poor little sister grieved; but she was forced to fetch the water, and the tears ran fast down her cheeks! 'Dear good God, help us now!' she exclaimed. 'Had we only been eaten by the wild beasts in the wood, then we should have died together.' But the old witch called out, 'leave off that noise; it will not help you a bit.'

So early in the morning Gretel was forced to go out and fill the kettle and make a fire. 'First we will bake, however,' said the old woman; 'I have already heated the oven and kneaded the dough;' and so saying, she pushed poor Gretel up to the oven, out of which flames were burning fiercely.

'Creep in,' said the witch, 'and see if it is hot enough, and then we will put in the bread.' But she intended, when Gretel got in, to shut up the oven and let her bake, so that she might eat her as well as Hansel. Gretel could tell what her thoughts were, and said, 'I do not know how to do it; how shall I get in?'

'You stupid goose,' said she, 'the opening is big enough. See, I could even get in myself!' and she got up and put her head into the oven. Then Gretel gave her a push, so that she fell right in, and then shutting the iron door, she bolted it. Oh! how horribly she howled; but Gretel ran away, and left the wicked witch to burn to ashes.

Now she ran to Hansel, and, opening his door, called out, 'Hansel, we are saved, the old witch is dead!' So he sprang out, like a bird out of his cage when the door is opened; and they were so glad that they fell into each other's arms, and kissed each other over and over again. And now, as there was nothing to fear, they went into the witch's house, where in every corner there were caskets full of pearls and precious stones.

'These are better than pebbles,' said Hansel, putting as many into his pocket as it would hold; while Gretel thought, 'I will take some home too,' and filled her apron full. 'We must be off now,' said Hansel, 'and get out of this enchanted forest;' but when they had walked for two hours they came to a large piece of water. 'We cannot cross,' said Hansel; 'I can see no bridge.

'And there is no boat either,' said Gretel, 'but there swims a white duck. I will ask her to help us over;' and she sang:

> 'Little duck, good little duck,
>   Gretel and Hansel, here we stand;
> There is neither stile nor bridge –
>   Take us on your back to land.'

So the duck came to them, and Hansel sat himself on, and bade his sister sit behind him. 'No,' answered Gretel, 'that will be too much for the duck; she shall take us over one at a time.' This the good little bird did, and when they had reached the other side safely, and had gone a little way, they came to a well-known wood, which they knew better every step they walked, and at last they perceived their father's house. Then they began to run, and, bursting into the house, they fell into their father's arms. He had not had one happy hour since he had left the children in the forest; and his wife was dead. Gretel shook her apron, and the pearls and precious stones rolled out upon the floor, and Hansel threw down one handful after the other out of his pocket. Then all their sorrows were ended for ever and ever.

The Seven Voyages of Sindbad

The First Voyage

LONG, long, ago, in the reign of the Caliph Haroun al Raschid, there dwelt in the city of Bagdad a poor man named Hindbad, who gained a living by carrying goods from place to place for other people; in fact, he was a porter.

Though, as a rule, he did not grumble with his lot, there were times when he was not content. One of these times happened to be, when, tired out by the weight of his load, he had sat down to rest outside the house of a very rich man whose name was Sindbad.

As the soft strains of music from the house reached his ears, and the scent of rare perfumes fell upon his senses, he was struck by the difference between his lot and that of the man whose name was so like his own.

'Why should I be so poor, and he so rich?' said Hindbad aloud; 'am I not as good a man as he?'

Sindbad, hearing the words without seeing the speaker, sent a servant to bring Hindbad before him, and the poor man, fearing he knew not what, went into the splendid hall where Sindbad was feasting with a number of his friends.

Pointing to a seat at his right hand, Sindbad gave his guest a share of the good things on the table, and the meal being at length finished, 'Tell me,' said he, 'why you were grumbling?'

'Pardon me, my lord,' replied Hindbad, 'I was weary and sad at heart.'

'Have no fear,' said Sindbad kindly, 'I do not blame you for your words; but, that you may know how hard I had to work to win the riches I now enjoy, let me tell you the story of my life.'

With these words he began as follows:

'When I was but a young man my father died, leaving me a very large fortune, nearly the whole of which I spent in enjoying myself. At last I began to think, unless I wished to become poor, I had better try to make some more money with the little left to me, so, having bought some goods, I set sail for the Persian Gulf, hoping to sell or exchange them at a profit.

The ship called at several small islands, where we did some good trading. One day, when the vessel could not move for want of wind to fill her sails, we saw what seemed to be a little green field peeping above the water. Thinking it very strange, a party of us rowed out to it, taking some wood for a fire, and food, so that we might hold a feast.

We had all landed, and were in the middle of our meal when we found to our horror that we were on the back of some huge sea-monster. The creature shook its great body, and lashed its tail so angrily that as many as could jumped into the boat, others into the sea, and soon all except myself were aboard the ship.

A fresh breeze had begun to blow, and the sails being set at once, away went the ship, leaving me still on the monster's back. Suddenly the huge creature dived under water, and I should have gone too, but that seizing a large piece of wood I kept myself afloat.

All through that day and through the night I was tossed about by the waves, but was at last thrown on to the shore of what was really an island. After a while the sun came out, warming me, and making me feel that if I wished to gain strength I must seek some food.

Dragging myself with great pain toward the middle of the island, I had the good fortune to find a few herbs. These I ate, drinking afterwards from a spring of clear, cool water.

Wishing to see on what sort of place I had been cast, I walked on until a man met me, who, hearing my strange story, took me to a cave in which were several other men. They were the servants of the ruler of the island, and had come to this part of it in order to fetch his horses back to the palace.

It was lucky for me that I met them that day; had it not been for this I should most likely have died, as I could never have found my way to the other side of the island, where the people lived, and to which the king's servants were returning next day.

They were very kind, giving me food to eat, and taking me with them when they set out on their journey. As soon as we reached the palace they took me before the king, who also treated me with great kindness. He listened to my story, pitied my sad state, and asked me to stay with him as long as I cared to.

Now the chief city of his kingdom, the city in which I made my home, was built on the seashore. Every day ships came to it from all parts of the world, and I, hoping to meet someone from my own town, spent a great deal of time watching these ships, and talking to the merchants who came and went in them.

I also grew friendly with some of the natives – Indians they were, and very wise persons; but I never forgot to pay a daily visit to the king, with whose chief men I had many pleasant talks about the way in which their country and my own were governed.

Hearing one day of the island of Cassel, and of the sounds of drums being beaten every night on the shore, I had a great wish to visit it, which I did, seeing many large and curious fishes on my voyage.

Shortly after my return from Cassel, the very ship in which I had set out from Bussorah, and which had sailed away leaving me struggling for life in the water, came into the harbour. Among the many bundles of goods brought from this vessel to the shore I saw those which I had bought, and on which my name was clearly written. But, on telling the captain my name, and that I wished to have my goods, he looked at me in surprise.

"How can you be Sindbad?" he asked, "when I myself saw him drowned. I fear you are not an honest man, though you look like one. I believe you are telling a lie in order to get these goods which do not belong to you."

I was at some pains to make him believe I spoke the truth, and, at last, on several of the sailors saying they were sure I was Sindbad, he let me have the goods.

Having looked through my bundle, I carried the very best of the goods to the kindly king, and asked him to take them as a gift. He seemed pleased with the gift, but not quite sure how I, a poor man cast up by the sea, had been able to get them.

I then told him of the coming of the ship, and the finding of my own bales of goods, on which he took my costly present with great pleasure, and gave me one worth far more in return. I next sold or exchanged the rest of my goods, and, having bidden his majesty good-bye, set sail for Bussorah, taking with me many articles made only on the island. These I sold for a large sum of money, for so much, indeed, that I had no further need to work.'

When Sindbad had finished the story of his first voyage, he ordered the band to play again, and spent the rest of the day with his guests. The poor porter, who never in all his life had been so well treated before, enjoyed himself greatly, and, when the rich man, on bidding him good-night, bade him come again the next day to hear more of his story, giving him at the same time a purse full of money, Hindbad was delighted at his good fortune.

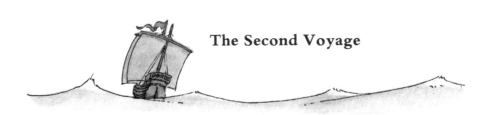

The Second Voyage

'Although I had made up my mind to live quietly at home on the money gained by my first voyage,' said Sindbad, when he and his poor guest were once more seated together, 'I soon tired of doing nothing, and having bought a large number of useful articles, once more set out to sell them to the people who lived on the various islands.

The ship carried us safely to several places where I sold my own goods and bought others; but one day we reached what seemed to be a desert island. No living creature was to be seen, yet there were fruit-trees and flowers, and meadows, and running streams, all of which looked so tempting, that we felt obliged to land, if only to walk a little in the pleasant-looking fields.

Having no wish to wander about with the rest, I took some food and wine, found a nice, shady spot beside a stream, ate a good meal, and then fell fast asleep, wakening only when the others had returned to the vessel, and sailed away without me.

I blamed myself over and over again for my stupidity, but, as this was not likely to help me much, I climbed a high tree in order to get a good view of the island. Far away in the distance I saw something white, and to this I went with all speed.

It was a curious thing, very large, very smooth, and rounded like a dome. While I stood wondering what it could be, all around grew dark. It was late in the day, and the sun would set in a little while, but the sky seemed to be hidden all at once by a thick cloud.

To my surprise this was not so, but the cloud was really a huge bird, bigger than I had ever dreamed a bird could be. I thought it must be the wonderful roc of which I had heard the sailors talk, and the great white dome must be its egg.

Thinking it likely the bird was coming to sit on her egg, I crept under it, and, as soon as she was settled, tied myself firmly to one of her big, strong legs.

Thus I lay until the morning, when the bird, rising high, carried me so swiftly through the air that I became dizzy, and lost my senses. On coming to myself some time later I was lying on the ground, but still tied to the leg of the huge bird.

Not wishing to go through such a terrible journey again, I made haste to get free from the bird's leg, and it was well I did so, for almost the next moment she seized a huge snake in her bill and flew away.

I could not tell where she had carried me. All around were mountains so high that they seemed to touch the sky, and so steep that no one could climb them. I was no better off here than on the island. Suddenly I forgot my trouble for a time, for, looking at the ground, I found it was covered with diamonds, big shining diamonds.

But, alas, there were other things besides, things that filled my heart with fear, and made me wish more than ever to find some way out of the lonely valley. These were snakes, so large that they could swallow an elephant quite easily.

As the day grew brighter, however, they hid away in their homes, for fear, I suppose, of the roc, but when the night drew near they came out again in large numbers. Feeling it would be dreadful to spend the dark night in terror in case I should be swallowed by one of the great creatures, I looked about for some place in which to take shelter till the day dawned.

At length I found a cave, the entrance to which was so small that I could block it with a large stone. Though now feeling safer I could still not sleep; the hissing of the snakes outside was too frightening.

As soon as it was light I left the cave, and walked a short distance through the valley, feeling far too miserable to touch the diamonds under my feet. The food I had brought from the ship kept me from starving, but I was so weary that at last I felt obliged to lie down and sleep.

Hardly had I begun to doze, however, when I was startled by something heavy falling near me. Opening my eyes quickly I saw a large piece of raw meat lying at my feet. Another piece fell, and another, and several more, and as they fell heavily upon the diamonds, the lovely stones stuck firmly into the meat.

This made me think again of the sailors' stories, and I knew that the meat was being thrown into the valley by men on the mountains, in the hope that it would be fetched back by the eagles to feed their young ones, when the diamonds could be taken from their nests.

Now I thought I could see a way of escape by tying a piece of meat firmly to my back, and waiting till an eagle carried me up out of the dreadful valley. This I did, but not until I had first filled my bag with the precious stones.

I had not long to wait. One of a number of eagles picking me up bore me to his nest on the top of the mountains, where I was found by a merchant who had frightened the eagle away. At first he looked at me in surprise, and then said I had no right to steal his diamonds.

"If you will listen to me," I said gently "you will find I am no thief, though having enough diamonds to make both myself and you rich for life. I got them from the valley, and chose the very best to be found."

The other merchants now crowded round, and all showed great surprise at my story. They wondered much at the trick I had played, but they wondered still more when I showed them the stones.

Though I begged him to take several, the merchant who had found me would take only the smallest of them, which he said was a good fortune in itself. They agreed to let me spend that night in their camp, which I did, and was then taken to the merchant's house, where I told my strange story again to his wife and children.

In the course of time I once more reached my home, and settled down to a life of ease, and made glad the hearts of my poor neighbours, by sharing my riches with them.'

This being the end of Sindbad's second story, he gave Hindbad another purse of money, and asked him to return the next day.

The Third Voyage

'My third voyage,' said Sindbad the next day, 'was hardly begun when a very great storm arose, and the captain told us the ship was being driven towards an island, which was the home of numbers of little hairy savages not more than a metre high. He said they were very fierce, and we had better not make them angry in case they became dangerous.

As our vessel neared the land a swarm of them swam out, dragged it ashore, made us all get out, and then took the ship away with them to another island. As it was useless to stand and look after them, we walked on until we reached a beautiful palace, the courtyard of which we entered.

The yard led to a room where we saw a heap of men's bones, and a large number of spits, or long, steel skewers, on which joints of meat are roasted. As we stood looking at these things, a truly terrible ogre came into the room, making a loud noise.

In the very middle of his forehead was a huge eye, the only one he had; his mouth was like that of a horse, and his ears flapped down on his shoulders like an elephant's. He was as tall as a high

tree, and one glance at him was enough to make us all nearly die with fright.

Having taken a good look at us, the horrid ogre picked me up by my neck, and turned me round and round, but seemed to think me too thin, for, indeed, I was little more than skin and bone. Then he seized the captain, who was the fattest of us all, roasted, and ate him.

After this he went to sleep, and troubled us no more till the next day, when he roasted and ate another of our crew. On the third day he ate another, and we then made up our minds to kill him and try to escape. There were ten of us left, and each one taking a spit, and making its point red hot, we stuck them all together into the one eye of our terrible enemy.

Mad with pain he tried to seize us; but we got out of the way of his fearful claw-like hands, and ran off to the shore. Here we made some rafts, but had not got afloat when two giants came in sight leading the terrible ogre who we had fondly hoped was dead.

Jumping on to the rafts we pushed off from the shore, but the giants wading into the water as far as they dared, threw after us some huge stones which, falling upon the rafts, sank them all but the one on which I stood with two other men. Happily we got out of their reach quickly and, after beating about on the sea for many hours, came to another island, where we found some very good fruit.

Being now tired out we lay down to sleep, but were soon awakened by a rustling sound which, to our horror, we found was made by a huge snake. Before we could get away, the creature swallowed one of my comrades, and then went back to his den. The next night he came again, and caught the second of my comrades, as he was following me up a tree, where he had hoped to be quite safe.

All night I lay on one of the boughs, afraid to sleep in case the cruel monster should come back. As soon as day broke I slid down, gathered all the brushwood near, and making it into bundles placed some of them round the tree; the others I tied to the topmost branches. When the sky began to darken in the evening, I lit them, and kept myself safe all night, for, though the snake came, he feared to cross my circle of fire.

In the morning, feeling very miserable, I made up my mind to drown myself, but, on reaching the shore, I saw some distance off a ship passing slowly by. Unrolling my turban I waved it aloft, while shouting loudly, until the captain sent a boat to fetch me to the ship.

Good fortune now met me once again, for this was the very captain who had sailed away without me on my second voyage. As soon as he learned who I was, he told me how glad he was to have been able to make up for that fault, by saving me now from what might have proved a worse fate.

He had taken care of my goods left on the ship, and now returned them to me with much pleasure. On reaching port I sold them at a fair price, and again returned to Bussorah with a large sum of money.

From Bussorah I went to Bagdad and bought another fine house with splendid grounds all round it. As I had done each time before, so I did now, giving a great deal of money to poor people of the city, and settling down for some time to a quiet life. But this I found very difficult to do, and at last went to sea for the fourth time, when again many wonderful things happened to me.'

Hindbad went home that night with a glad heart, for he was no longer poor. In his hand he held a purse of money, and it seemed as if his rich friend meant to give him the same, every day he spent with him.

The Fourth Voyage

As soon as dinner was over, Sindbad began the story of his fourth voyage. 'Having set all my affairs straight,' he said, 'I travelled through a great part of Persia, buying and selling. At last, reaching the coast, I went aboard a ship, which, after calling at several places on the mainland, stood out to sea.

But soon a great storm arose; the sails were torn to shreds, the ship was blown upon the land, and many of the passengers and sailors were drowned.

With a few of the others I clung to a plank, which was washed ashore on an island, where we found fruit and water, of which we ate and drank freely. The next morning we set out to explore the island, but before getting far were met by some islanders who carried us to their homes.

They seemed very kind and gave us a tasty dish to eat.

Though feeling as hungry as my comrades, I ate none of this dish, fearing it might do me some harm. In this I was wise, for I was the only one who kept his senses. The others became dazed, and ate freely of the rice with which they were daily fed, becoming at last very fat, when the islanders killed and ate them.

The horror of the whole thing, together with the very little food I ate, kept me so thin that the islanders took no notice of me, which gave me the chance of going here and there without being watched. One day, when all the people except one old man had gone out, I walked slowly till some distance away from the village, when I set off running as fast as I could, taking no notice of the old man's cries.

Resting a while now and then, I hurried on until night came. For seven days I met no one; on the eighth I had the good fortune to come upon some men gathering pepper, which was plentiful on the island. On hearing my story they seemed very much surprised that I had got away with my life.

They treated me with much kindness and, when their work was done, took me with them to their own island, where the king gave me some new clothes and bade his people take great care of me. I became a great favourite with every one, and at last found a way of paying back a little of their kindness.

Seeing that all of them, even the king, rode upon the bare backs of their horses, I thought out a plan for making a saddle and bridle and stirrups. This, with the help of two workmen, I did, and gave the first set, when finished, to the king. So many costly presents were given me by those for whom I made saddles that I was soon a rich man again.

One day the king, as a token of his love, gave me a wife, thinking I should be more likely to settle down in his country, and not wish to return to my own. At first I was pleased enough to stay, but after a time I began to long for my own home in Bagdad. Therefore, keeping my eyes open, I waited for a chance to escape, which came about in a very curious manner.

My wife, who for some time had not been strong, fell sick and died, when, according to the custom of the country, I was buried with her in a deep pit on the side of a mountain near the sea.

My coffin was an open one, and when the mouth of the pit had been blocked by a huge rock, and the king with the other mourners had gone away, I rose, and by the aid of a little light that came through the corners not covered by the stone, looked about me.

The pit or long cave, as it really was, seemed full of dead bodies, which smelt so horribly that I was forced to hold my nose. At first I wished I had died in one of the storms at sea; then I was filled with a keen desire to live. Taking some of the bread and water placed in the coffin, I groped about to find some outlet from the cave, but failed to do so.

My food was nearly all gone, when, one day, the mouth of the cave was uncovered, and I saw another burial taking place. The dead body was that of a man, and his wife being buried with him, the usual seven small loaves and a pitcher of water had been placed in her coffin. The poor woman, however, soon died, so I took the bread and water, which lasted me for several days.

Then, one morning, hearing a strange sound, I was able to follow it, until I came upon an opening in the cave, through which I crawled, and found myself on the seashore. The sound I had heard proved to be the heavy breathing of some creature that had come into the cave to feed upon the dead bodies.

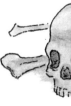

Feeling sure now of being able to get away from my living tomb, I went back to the cave in order to get the precious stones, and jewels, and costly stuffs buried with the dead bodies, and also to bring away my bread and water. On again reaching the shore I made several neat bundles of the goods, and then settled down to wait for the passing of some ship in the hope of being picked up.

On the third day, a vessel sailed slowly out from the harbour, and I, waving the linen of my turban, shouted loudly, which at last caused the sailors to look toward me. In a few minutes a boat was lowered and three men rowed ashore to fetch me.

To account for being in so strange a place, I told them I had been shipwrecked, but had got safely to land with a portion of my goods. The story was really a very poor one, but they seemed not to notice it, being far too busy with their own affairs.

The ship called at several ports on the islands and the mainland, where I made another large fortune by the sale of the articles brought from the cave, and at length I reached my home in safety.

As an act of thankfulness for having come safely through my troubles, I gave large sums of money to the church, to the poor, and to my own kindred, who listened in wonder to the story of my latest adventures.'

Here Sindbad wished his guests good-night, bidding them all dine with him next day, and giving Hindbad the usual purse of one hundred sequins.

The Fifth Voyage

'The pleasures of my home,' said Sindbad the next evening, 'made me forget past dangers, so, when the longing for travel came upon me, I bought many costly articles with which to carry on my trade, and sent them to the seaport town where a vessel was being built for my use.

The ship being larger than I needed for my own goods, I agreed to take several other merchants with me, and we set out in great hope of doing good business at the ports where we meant to call.

But, alas! coming one day to a desert island, where we found a young roc just ready to break from its shell, the merchants roasted and ate it, and thus brought about the deaths of every one except myself.

Just as my comrades had finished their meal, for I would by no means join in it, we saw the parent birds coming. The captain, fearing the anger of the great creatures, who looked like two large clouds floating in the sky, hurried us aboard and sailed away with all speed.

As soon as the old birds found what had been done, they swept down with a great noise, took up two huge stones, and flew after us. Stopping just above us they dropped the stones, one of which fell upon the ship, smashing it to pieces, and killing most of the sailors and merchants. Some, myself among them, sank into the water.

On coming to the surface I caught hold of a plank with one hand, and swam with the other, changing them at times, until the tide carried me to an island, the shore of which was so steep that some further toil was needed before I reached a place of safety.

In the morning, after eating the fruits which grew in plenty, and drinking the fresh, cool water of a brook, I wandered about, looking with pleasure at the beauty of the place.

After a time I saw a little old man making signs to me to carry him on my back over the brook. Having pity on his age, I did so, but, when I would have pulled him down on the other side, he twisted his legs so tightly round my neck, that I fell to the ground half choked.

Though he saw how faint I was he made no sign of getting off, but, opening his legs a little to let me breathe better, he dug his feet into my stomach to make me rise and carry him farther. Day after day, and night after night, he clung to me, until by good luck I got rid of him.

Coming to a spot where, a few days before, I had left the juice of some grapes in a container, I drank the juice which in the meantime had become very good wine. This gave me fresh strength, and, instead of dragging myself wearily along, I danced and sang with great good-will.

The old man, seeing how light-hearted the wine had made me, signed to me to give him some. He took a deep drink, and soon became so merry that he loosed his hold on my shoulders, when I tossed him off, and stunned him with a stone, in case he should make me his victim once more.

Some sailors whom I met shortly afterwards, their ship having put into the island for water, said I was the first person they had ever known to escape from the old man of the sea, who for years had been a terror to those obliged to visit the island.

One of the merchants on board, taking pity on my state, gave me a large bag, and advised me to go picking cocoa-nuts with some men whom we met in a place much visited by foreign traders. I kept close to the party, as he had bidden me, until we reached the place where the cocoa-nuts grew.

The trees were so tall that I wondered how we should get the nuts, when the men, picking up some stones, threw them at the monkeys of whom there were many on the branches. These creatures in return, pelted us with cocoa-nuts, throwing them down so quickly that we soon filled our bags.

Day after day this was done until at length we had enough to fill the ship which waited for us in the harbour. Then, bidding the friendly merchant good-bye, I went aboard, and in due time arrived in Bagdad, none the worse for my adventures. I had done well, too, with my cocoa-nuts, having changed them for pearls and spices in the places at which we had called.'

Giving Hindbad another hundred sequins, Sindbad wished him goodnight, and asked him to return next day to hear the story of his sixth voyage.

The Sixth Voyage

'You will perhaps wonder why, after meeting with so many dangers, I should again venture forth, when I might have stayed quietly at home,' said Sindbad, taking up his story where he had left off the day before. 'I wonder myself, now, yet at the time I was quite willing and eager to set out.

Travelling by way of Persia and the Indies, I at length took passage on a vessel bound on a long voyage. After being many days at sea the captain and pilot lost their way. They had no idea where we were, until the captain found his ship had got into a most dangerous current which, unless God took pity on us, would surely carry us to our death.

Almost mad with grief he left his place on deck, and went to see that his orders were carried out; but, as the men set about changing the sails, the ropes broke, and the vessel, now quite helpless, was carried ashore and wrecked, yet not so badly, for we were able to save our lives, our goods, and our provisions.

But even such comfort as was left us was taken away by the captain. 'We may as well set about digging our graves,' said he, 'for no one ever escapes from this terrible place.'

And, indeed, this seemed true, the shore being covered with wrecks, and goods of great value, and, worst of all for men in our position to see, the bones of those who had already died there, as we were only too likely to do.

The coast was very steep, and there seemed no way of climbing up, but under the hills, through a great cave, ran the very current that had brought us ashore. For some days we wandered about, heedless of the precious stones under our feet, thinking only of our sad fate. The most careful ate only a little of their share of food each day, so that some lived longer than others; but at last I was the only one left, and, maddened by my foolishness in leaving home, I began to dig my grave, fully believing that now at least there was no more hope.

Yet it pleased God again to spare me. As I stood, lonely and miserable, looking upon the currents that had wrought our ruin, an idea came into my head. With all speed I made a raft with the pieces of timber on the shore, loaded it with the precious stones

and costly stuffs lying here and there, and stepped aboard, trusting that the stream would carry me to some place where men lived, and so give me a chance of escape. If I lost my life, I should be no worse off than in staying on the coast to die.

With two small oars I guided the raft, leaving it to be carried by the current. Several days passed, and still the raft floated on in total darkness through the long tunnel. At length my food being all eaten, I sank down in a state of drowsiness, and awoke to find myself once more in the light, and surrounded by a number of black men.

Full of joy at my good fortune I rose, and gave thanks aloud to God, who had brought me to a place of safety. One of the blacks, understanding my words, stepped forward and asked how I had reached their country. They had seen my raft floating in the river, he said, and had tied it to the bank till I should awake. After eating a little food I told them of my strange adventures, the man who had first spoken to me telling the others what I said, he being the only one who understood my speech.

They looked at me in wonder, and placing me on a horse took me straight to their king. He thought my story so strange that he had it written down in letters of gold, and put away with the important papers of the kingdom. The sight of my raft and bales of goods, which the natives had taken care to bring with them, was a still further surprise. He thought my treasures very beautiful, but most of all the emeralds, of which he himself had none.

Seeing this, I begged him to accept the whole of my goods, as a token of my thankfulness to him and his people, but this he would by no means do. He said that instead of taking my riches he meant to add to them, and meanwhile, I was placed in the care of one of his chief men, who treated me with great kindness.

Though the time passed pleasantly, I could not but long to return to my home. Going therefore to pay my daily visit to the king, I told him of my wish, and begged that he would let me return to Bagdad. He agreed at once, and, giving me many valuable gifts, asked that I would carry a message of friendship to the Caliph Haroun al Raschid, together with a costly present, and a letter written upon a skin of great value. Then, sending for the captain in whose ship I was to sail, and the merchant who was to travel with me, he charged them to treat me well on the journey.

Reaching Bagdad in the course of time, I set out to fulfil my promise to the king. His gift to the Caliph was made up of four things – a beautiful cup cut out of a large ruby and filled with pearls; the skin of a snake supposed to keep any one who lay upon it from becoming ill; a large quantity of wood of aloes, and of camphor; and a beautiful slave whose clothing was rich with jewels.

The Caliph, astonished at the richness of the gift, could not keep from asking many questions about the king who had given it into my care. After telling him all he wished to know, I was free to return home, and to settle down again, this time, as I thought, for good.'

The story being finished, Hindbad went away, taking with him another purse of gold; but the next day he returned to dine with Sindbad, who, after the meal, told the story of his seventh and last voyage in these words.

The Seventh Voyage

'I was one day enjoying myself with some friends, when a slave from the palace came with a message that I should go to the Caliph at once. His Highness, having written a reply to the letter from the King of the Indies, wished me to carry it to him, together with a suitable present.

Now, though it would have given me great pleasure to serve my sovereign in any other way, I felt quite unable to face again the dangers of the sea, and, to let him know why, I told him of all the misery through which I had passed. In reply he said that though he felt very sorry for me, yet I must bear this letter and gift to the King of the Indies.

"You have but to sail to Serendib," said he, "and present my gifts to his Majesty: after that you are free to return to Bagdad."

Seeing that he would not change his mind, I at last agreed to go, and, after a fair and pleasant voyage, arrived at the king's court. The gift was a very costly one, and his Majesty showed great pleasure when it was handed to him.

After a short stay in the island I begged leave to depart, but the king gave his consent only after much pressing on my part. I went on board the vessel, taking with me a splendid gift, and hoping to have a speedy and pleasant voyage.

We had been at sea, however, only about three days, when the ship being seized by pirates, I was taken with several others and sold as a slave. The rich merchant, who bought me, treated me well, and, finding I was able to shoot with a bow, took me out with him to shoot elephants of which there were numbers in the forest.

Having told me to climb a tree and to wait for the animals to pass by, he gave me a supply of food, and went back to the town.

No elephants passed during the night, but in the morning I shot one out of a large herd. As soon as the others had gone, I ran quickly to my master, who, praising me highly, came back to the forest and helped to bury the huge creature. This he did to get the tusks, when the flesh had rotted away from them.

Every day for two whole months I shot an elephant; then one morning as I waited in the tree for them, instead of passing by they came toward it, and looked at me steadily for a few moments. I trembled with fear, for the creatures were many in number, and seemed bent on taking my life in revenge for the death of their friends.

One great animal at last tore up the tree in which I was by the roots, lifted me from the ground where I had fallen, placed me

on his back, and, closely followed by the others, carried me to a field, some distance away, which I found afterwards to be covered with the bones and teeth of dead elephants.

Having laid me on the ground they all went away, leaving me lost in wonder at their wisdom. It seemed as if they knew it was only their teeth I wanted, and they had brought me to their burying-place, so that I could get all I wished without killing any more of their number.

Here, indeed, was a great treasure, and I went quickly to tell my master of my good fortune. As I met no elephants on the way, I felt sure they had gone farther into the forest in order to leave the road open. My master, wondering why I was so long away, had meanwhile gone to the tree and found it torn from the ground, so he was overjoyed to see me, having feared the creatures had killed me in their anger.

The next day we rode to the spot on an elephant whom we loaded with as many tusks as it could carry, and on getting back home my master said that as he had become a rich man through me, I should be a slave no longer.

"The merchants of this city," he said, "have had many slaves killed by the elephants, who are indeed very cunning animals. But it has pleased God to spare your life, and to show how every one of us may become rich without the loss of any more lives. I have no doubt that when the people of this city hear about this they will all wish to help in making you a rich man, but I would rather do this by myself. I will not only set you free, I will give you enough money to live on for the rest of your life."

Having thanked the merchant for his kindness, I said, "Sir, I have no wish to take so great a gift from you. Give me leave to return to my own country a free man, and I shall be well content."

This he was quite willing to do, saying that as soon as the wind was fair, he would send me home in one of the ships that would then come to carry away the ivory.

While waiting for the ships I made several journeys to the hill with the friendly merchant, bringing home so many tusks that the storehouses were soon full of ivory. The vessels came at last, and the merchant himself, choosing the one in which I was to sail, filled it with ivory, the half of which he said was mine. Besides this splendid present he gave me a number of things found or made only in that island, and enough food to last the whole voyage: he also paid the cost of my journey.

The voyage was a good one, yet, knowing the dangers of the ocean, and how quickly storms arise, I landed at the first port we reached on the mainland, taking with me my share of the ivory which soon sold for a great deal of money.

Having bought some rare gifts for my family, I set out for Bagdad with a party of merchants. The way was long and tiring, but reaching the city at length, I went straight to the Caliph, in order to let him know that his commands had been properly carried out.

I had been so long away that he feared some danger had befallen me, so I made bold to tell him of my adventures. The story of the elephants filled him with wonder; indeed, had he not known me to be a truthful man, he would not have believed it.

As it was he gave orders that this story, as well as all the others I had told, should be written in letters of gold, and kept in a safe place for all time.

My family, my kindred, and all my friends welcomed my return with great joy. Since that, my last voyage, I have lived a quiet life, doing much good.'

'Now, friend,' he added, turning to Hindbad, 'I think you will agree I have earned the riches I enjoy, and the pleasures that fill my life.'

'Sir,' replied Hindbad, as he rose and kissed his host's hand, 'I must own that your troubles have been greater than mine. You richly deserve all you have, and I hope you will from now live a happy and peaceful life.'

Although he had no more stories to tell, Sindbad begged the poor porter to come to dine with him every day. 'You need not do any more rough work,' said he, wishing him good-night, and putting into his hand another full purse, 'for Sindbad the Sailor will be your friend for the rest of your life.'

The Cat & the Fox

A CAT and a fox were exchanging views upon the difficulties of living in peace and safety from those who were always ready to take their lives.

'I do not care a bit for any of them,' said the fox at last. 'Things may be very bad, as you say, but I have a thousand tricks to show my enemies before they can do me harm.'

'You are fortunate,' replied the cat. 'For my part, I have only one way of evading my enemies, only one method of escape and if that fails all is lost.'

'I am sorry for you with all my heart,' said Reynard. 'If one could tell a friend from a foe in these difficult times, I would show you one or two of my tricks.'

Hardly had he finished speaking when a pack of hounds burst suddenly upon them.

The cat, resorting to her single trick, ran up a tree, and from the security of the topmost branches witnessed the downfall of the braggart.

Unable to make up his mind which of the thousand tricks he would adopt the fox was quickly caught before he could put even one of them into operation.

Pride goes before a fall.

The Arab & the Camel

A N Arab, having loaded his camel, asked him whether he preferred to go uphill or downhill.

'Why do you ask, master?' said the camel dryly. 'Is the level way across the plain shut up?'

What use is it to pretend there is a choice when there is none?